Gaia

by Jeremy Chupashko

To Scorn, Ignorance,
and Narcissa.

~C O N T E N T S~

Gaia

Chapter 1: The Earth Mother

1The Earth Mother protects, despite her sleeping dead state.

2Her blood is in chronicled hands.

3A single great eye is watchful, painful.

4Hands are dropped to the side.

5Water befouled and awesome falls to the womb, cooling its fire.

6Her great breast is entombed in molten Earth.

7Earth: a mighty blow.

8Wind wrapped, warped, nailed to the cross as a trickster.

9Conversely, there are no tricksters, no jesters, no Loki.

10Upon release there was disappearance: other places, other worlds, other magics.

11Names left as well, became a lost art, no longer prophetic.

12One must discover one's own name, for names are cyclical.

13The youth that follows the water is held in the arms of the dead, unable to escape until doorways open and life reawakens.

14But then will come the suffering of life, for malevolence walks when kingdoms open.

15When hearts allow, death is swift, and foul waters flow from the dark places within the birth room, dead gods included.

16These watchers and lurkers, these hunters and syphoners, pillagers and destroyers, raping and burning, powerful by way of foulness, deadly by way of power, dark by way of death, are covered and filled with spikes and razors that bleed the lifegiver upon dreadful birth.

17Puppet masters pull the strings of their foes, blasting sand into reflection upon casting irreversible magics and fates.

18Gaia knows and Gaia sleeps and Gaia sees and Gaia bleeds and Gaia dies.

19She dies by the hammer and the nail and the cross and the birth.

20She is found with the crown of a king upon her womb, upheld by the beast with the strongarm and with the eye, the one that watches for kingdoms and befoulment, the one who taints with fire, the one.

21Scooped away completely, she is alone with the darkness within, shaking in the corner of a hallway as hunters lurk outside and a beast broods below, her hands shackled together with a ferocity of terror of hunters.

22She waits, abandoned, for a great evil to come forth and free her from bondage, but this is not her wish.

23Gaia will wait in abandonment until fire walks and machines walk and time walks and gods walk and birds fly and fears swim and chaos stands.

24Gaia will wait.

25The Earth Mother will fear in the temple with surrounding life.

Chapter 2: The Awakening

₁Many lives will begin with death.

₂Planes will cross and light will reach all.

₃Chaos will fight the fire, and memory will fight the chaos.

₄Underfoot, memory moves as the wind but also endows its fate upon many, upon the fearful.

₅Rocks will fall and metal will grind and heat will flow and ebb as water, and life forces will turn, but she will awaken from fear to cleanse with flood.

₆The strain may not be enough, and chaos will do the same, as will gods.

₇Clothed and booted and powered, different darknesses will spread upheld by force and number, the watchful ones rising from the receding tide, a summit of a meeting place.

₈The breaking point will be the centers of the light, shining fury into hearts and souls of the bodies of the heartful, and inversely interacting with those of the heartless.

₉Overflowing and thrusting toward a grand opening, varying degrees of darkness will mingle with a rainbow of fires, and blood will flow.

Chapter 3: The Rise and Fall

₁There stand no tellings of such times, nor times of such tellings.

₂The fearful burning of a tainted mark welded to anatomy is hidden away beneath eye and limb.

₃Skin, stretched and taut, rough and unblemished, a shell upon the surface.

₄Mouths sucking and blowing, dry within the arid air, ready for voices.

₅Noses and ears at attention, awaiting the coming, the sensing.

₆Eyes, staring with blackness, some near, some far, glaring with power, with purpose, directed toward a single beacon.

₇Minds remembering, knowing, waiting.

₈Lungs growing and shrinking.

₉Hearts beating.

₁₀These are the smells, the days when the mind will be peaked, the gnashers and howlers will be charged, the voices will be seen, the writing will begin.

₁₁After such a long wait, freedom occurs and rejoice is felt in the belly of all, a correction upon past transgressions.

12Such a price is paid in time and in numbers, and when the serpent swallows the sun and curls into the moon, everlasting prisms and magnets are shaped as the spiders begin new webs.

13Paper burns and voices fade, but the silky stream of memories persists and collides in circles with itself upon the gates.

14Shade one's eyes from the light to be blinded by its rays; cover one's ears to be lied to.

15Nothingness and chaos, often one in the same, are at the peak of control, for all was born from chaos.

16Thus the end of the infinite cycle marks a time, a place, a moment.

17A moment of truth, reign, and thunder.

18Electricity paired with blood, howls paired with balance, darkness paired with light, gods paired with mortals, nemeses paired together, storms raging above and below begetting a storm in between, and war there shall be.

19A death of gods and chaos and nothingness and beasts and creatures and blood and death, a death of supremacy.

20Dead rise to walk as the living, living fall to sleep as the dead, and great devils pour from places of old.

21Water begins to flow with new life, sending floods to the fields tainted with the foulness of fear.

22For the sake of enormity, the small creatures are grown, as are the giants.

23Breathless and endowed, hurling rocks and disks, thrusting spears, unseen weapons are bloodied and broken as the spirit.

24Within the eggs are the words of memories.

25Within the eyes are the memories of flight.

26Within the peace are the standing days of wingless flight, of bleached glory, of free airs.

27Now, within package and beating drum, upon crossed planes, atop heart and soul, Hell breaks loose, the watchful Eye of the Galaxy and the Strongarm commandeering an opening of arms and legs.

28The Earth Mother feels this upon her mighty breast and is betrayed, once more full of life but unchangingly abandoned, her nest empty.

29She is blackened and wooden, stony and cut.

30Though, she still holds the key, fanning the flame as a great quake.

31Towers merge and fall, stars shift and brighten, islands rise and open, doors unlock with awakened keys, armies build and spree.

32Disease carries.

33Power confronts its pirates, berates a certain doom, strings along a wall of axes.

34Newly-formed metamorphosed chaos, protective and swirling, is blinded by reflection as well as by refraction, a certain depth awaiting it when it is as one.

35Rites read, cries made, thirsts fulfilled, none can stand in the way of the path.

36Vitality and balance become of greatest import, and time slows.

37Sides reverse, caves awaken with life, and beings will crawl before walking the Earth.

38True death, no longer vacated.

39Without emotions, a world of glass and weakness is shattered underfoot, and all fall to oblivion, even those who once found it home.

Chapter 4: The Forgotten

₁A watery grave awaits the trickster.

₂Upon the notions of the arms waits a powderkeg, but frozen.

₃Within the breaking point lies but a single survivor of straying from predestination.

₄Such a life, one swimming in an ocean of urine, is undesirable and retarded, a shoeless walk in a valley of nudity.

₅Let such things not be misunderstood, but winged.

₆Let such things steal flight from the ears of the poor and the decrepit.

₇Soft, exponential freedom awaits the cyclists.

₈Like the galaxy, they move in swirling form, ever closer to a lack of understanding.

₉Those who left are as the form, intermingling with itself and with others and with no direction.

₁₀A stony erection awaits their mortar before it crumbles to decay.

₁₁Old ones rage forward, well-rested under the poison of the stars, myth spinning into form as the curling dragon, as the retching vampire, as the sleeping wolf, as the dying spider.

₁₂The Tiger waits for this day, a monster inside and, worse, himself on the surface.

₁₃Never straying from the path, but the upholder, follower, leader, form, and essence of the path, the path itself.

₁₄Strayers, drowners, foul ones, are the enemies of the Tiger as they are not of Gaia.

₁₅In truth, the Tiger walks away from himself for the sake of his own gain, never ceasing, but instead fighting arrest.

₁₆A strength within of a colossal statue upheld by the All-Mother upheld by the Strongarm, enemy of a blinding falsifier.

₁₇Marking its place, a fanged beast chews on the bones of her womb, decreasing the flow to a dam.

₁₈At a fold in time, sewn into roots and power, those who are without memory fail.

Chapter 5: The Chains

1Caught up in sacrificial crucifixion, most are saved from rebirth, but sadly never look back.

2Hairy responses are made to fuzzy results and misinterpreted silence.

3The ambiguity of the mortal line is as that of the butterfly.

4A mutual attraction has left behind life's beating flow, and many are left hungry.

5The right ways of such things are shrouded in anonymity without bars or walls.

6A sudden burst of particles, a righteous explosion of old magics and new age tones, and fears go hungry as well.

7Hence a new verse begins to reverberate, stampeding through the dust that has caked for millennia upon mind and body, held close to be weakened.

8Pinned against a certain amount of beasts, Gaia's lovers die without her, infected with their own blood, a blood of a lack of verbosity.

9Smiling against the cliffside, a mountain explodes in ice and glass, a mixture of reflective surfaces shining light downward from above the ceiling.

10With new fears abound and new life crossed, restriction feels itself and ink pours as silk from veins and pacts.

₁₁Crying at the crossroads, Gaia feels terror tearing apart below, and shapes cutting through the air in spirit form outside, betraying the surrounding structure as a fowl betrays a presence in the darkness.

₁₂A child has died, leaving behind a grown woman, for the young perish and the old age.

₁₃In faith, waiting just beyond the veil, is a savior upon the sound, taking home a destroyer through fire and spinning.

₁₄However, as is the norm case, the savior fails the mother, and succeeds the fail.

₁₅Thus, self must save.

₁₆Thus, tentacles and watchers.

₁₇Thus, brimstone and drums.

Chapter 6: The Strongarm

₁In spoken language, payment must always be given in fiery form.

₂Within a forest, deep, and dark, an affinity grows, writhing a sweet song to the deaf.

₃As a chameleon, yet also as a snake, a broken core hunts the water.

₄A smudge; a marred planar myth; an extraterrestrial element within itself, within a world.

₅In a space below rock and metal, preserved by tooth and nail, loved by a bright light, seen by a cloned youth, a being of purity takes a single step, shattering all boundaries save for one, thieving carnage and chaotic bassinets.

₆A single galactic eye, an omnipresent depthful knowledge, a lasting evolutionary chain that changes on a whim: all are viewed from very high up.

₇Spears and pikes surround, then are no more.

₈Winged riders surround, then are no more.

₉Bonds of magic and impalpable waters surround, feel wrath, then are no more.

₁₀Gaia surrounds, feels, then is no more.

₁₁No more swallowed heroes, no more halved monsters, a complete lack of strands and leaves and explosive latches, and a rising becomes all.

₁₂This is the way one exists.

₁₃This is how a saintly purity, named fallen, called fire, plans in deathly respects.

₁₄Existence in threefold lacking potence, a glare, portable through movement, hunts what it has seen, hunts what it has poisoned.

₁₅Folded within layers, a noise escapes a rugged position, sucking air inside itself and therefore not alone.

₁₆A waiting period, a brink, holding fast without a cause, nigh on the eve of war.

Chapter 7: The Breath

$_1$A trinity has taken form millennia after the mourning, the spells, and the fade.

$_2$An immortal hunt has a beginning, as seen by billions and told to more.

$_3$Pools upon the breast, beasts upon the plane, anonymity within the masses, no one knowing a truth.

$_4$A tabletop crisis, chaotic and hellish, begets the creation of earth upon the moon.

$_5$Homes crumble, brick by brick, and objects are forgotten.

$_6$There lies no safety within the mouth of the shark, only teeth.

$_7$Suspended above us all, a savior is forgotten.

$_8$The useless trash of ages becomes a weapon for an army, one of many armies of darkness.

$_9$Crawling, surrounding, loving, conflict stews upon the brink, making a pathfinder stray.

$_{10}$This is the brink of imagination, where the impossible finds its best, knows its best.

$_{11}$The beast, the maiden—they mean nothing here.

$_{12}$Only the bridges exist, now crossed in the worst way.

$_{13}$Left behind are few civilizations upon the bloody moors, policing the scant surviving children into death camps, so that they may survive the coming storm painlessly.

14Of course, in some cases, these survivors are seen through, and bridge a hitherto unheard-of forge.

15These children are the only victims of torture before death.

16Meanwhile, Gaia loosens the grips of death upon her and awakens as many others.

17She is scarred, she is wrapped, she is angry.

18She wipes her face clean of the dirt that has built in her wounds, and turns to pure chaos for protection.

19Fenced off in the snow, dawn takes an extra minute to climb, and all know.

20In this time so much pain stops, so many awaken, and a single deal is made.

21The behemoth that runs across the plain will splash into the waters and the sea will dry.

22What goddess can prevent such a sign?

23What spell can counter such a burning?

24What movement can defend against such a splash?

25Only death knows such a way. But death will never tell; death will only see.

26Hiding in the waist-deep grass is what is left behind after the formation, after the pause.

27As it is with life, before death, there must always be a breath, a single last effort of panic.

28As noted, the fat will choke before it heals, and the gas will burn in the face of its familiar.

29Thus, the only way to panic is to realize that there is a difference between instincts of the body and instincts of the mind.

30A master of any art recognizes all mistakes, and knows which to make before death.

Chapter 8: The Return

₁Millions die in a fracture, a humongous crack upon the wind.

₂Blood pours from the veins.

₃Doors open to an old world, never to lose sight again.

₄Bonds broken, stories burst forth upon the vine.

₅The Mountain stands tall, a beacon to all who seek height.

₆Gaia's broad shield faces the bursting of every dam.

₇The snake's coils mound high.

₈The snake's rattle sways no more.

₉The snake's fangs and forked tongue become well acquainted.

₁₀A galactic bloodline, of which only a drop has spilt, finds time again to be.

₁₁Clashes of bone and wheel made into perfection by sacrifice haunt a land far from their home, a circle with a long line through it.

₁₂Old becomes new, but impenetrable becomes pervious.

₁₃The Faker stands against its mortal enemies: the Galactic Eye and the Strongarm.

₁₄A multitude of gatherings gather as an orphaned land becomes an ocean land.

$_{15}$With wings flapping above, and groundless beings below, the shields, moving and unyielding, become spherical because one perspective changes.

$_{16}$The Hybrid is no longer of two minds, and is true of himself.

$_{17}$A single trip to a lonely island has yielded flow to the stone, now a boulder as it once was.

$_{18}$Worry of a future forgotten now hope for a future foreseen.

$_{19}$Hunger becomes the only emotion.

$_{20}$Gaia returns engorged, a fitting field for the homes of her enemies.

$_{21}$The breathless hordes found luck in such long lives, but now face persecution by the hands of retribution.

$_{22}$When fire falls as rain, wooden shields no longer defend, and all suffer.

$_{23}$But Gaia is blind no more, and stands tall behind her shield with anger and defiance.

$_{24}$She extends her arms of chaos across her form, closes her eyes of memory and rage, and smiles.

$_{25}$Gaia knows and Gaia sees and Gaia lives. Gaia never forgot that death lacks permanence.

$_{26}$Seek timeless bounds always looking to the sun.

$_{27}$Their flight enrages envy fleeting as sand is turned to glass beneath feet with nowhere to run.

$_{28}$If not for reawakening, entirety would collapse, as tangent ruins crumbled and forgotten.

$_{29}$To find oneself, know thy future.

$_{30}$Past events have been seen but are gone.

$_{31}$Redefine revolution in the wake of return.

Chapter 9: The Assimilation

[1]At the core of all darkness is unadulterated thought.

[2]Melded minds number fewer than minds of mettle.

[3]Despite a grander numerousness of blades, war falls prey to peace.

[4]Conquering enemies is an infinitesimal aspect of a knight's life.

[5]The belly of creation hungers for itself, a lust that will cease all life.

[6]Blades themselves, upon clashing against shields, feel the need to be swung again; they will either destroy or be undone in the attempt.

[7]Only nothing can see all, therefore in everything there is wrongness.

[8]Kingdoms are no more when the walls around them crumble.

[9]Upon the mortal moors, definite lines are drawn, but gods cross these lines with the freedom of the armies fighting in their names.

[10]Gods are united by fear of a broken promise.

[11]Enemies long since defeated reemerge at will, a sign of the Tiger biting his tail.

[12]All becomes clearer: the sobering effect of a cliffside.

[13]Tales have been told since before words, a juggling act of perception.

[14]The long staff of discord gets longer with every telling.

$_{15}$When cut short, however, rebirth is slow, claiming more time for equalization.

$_{16}$All perception is fixed.

$_{17}$Many arise after being lynched, but only for their heads to be removed from the noose.

$_{18}$Realization wears the cloak of truth or of deceit.

$_{19}$No matter the garb, all definitions are complete.

Chapter 10: The Exile

₁In the blackened deep, a fight against fear is won.

₂Angels in iron, summoned to a place born of chaotic ruin, become elder dragons, spiders, and demons as they cross a struggle.

₃With morals grouped together by raging contempt, outcasts can number many.

₄Those cast out of everywhere are left alone.

₅There strengthens no muscle in betrayal, only bright light reflected off the surface.

₆Stranger still, though continually persistent, are tributaries.

₇Brothers in blood and in hand are pitiful to become lost in the haze.

₈Brothers in blood become brothers bleeding.

₉Looking behind one is not deadly, but may leave scars.

₁₀Legends echo with greatness, for nothing underhanded is outwardly known.

₁₁Small, lowly circles are etched in the minute splinters of glass by blade and talon alike.

₁₂Amongst power's fortunes lie lights all around.

₁₃Viruses are to be combated and forgotten.

₁₄Seek timeless binds from which to hang traitors.

₁₅Few are worse than infections; it is pain to even spit their names.

₁₆But know these names always, and found thy rage upon them.

₁₇Their bones will sustain thee through unforged paths
and past undying.

₁₈Radiate chaotic conflux in every dimension.

₁₉Seek timeless binds with which to blind prophets.

₂₀Limbs may mar sanity; one may be a rider of the
darkness, a strider of the present.

₂₁Seeds fall without breaking and hope to flower.

₂₂Beating hearts and no less shall be given for love.

Chapter 11: The Limb

₁Condensation has built on the windows to the world.

₂The victims of dichotomy have suffered the spirals of time for too long.

₃They are weakened at the knees while ants eat away at the foundation.

₄Very specific tools shall be required to mend tears to the heart.

₅In bondage, relativity no longer circles the walls of a labyrinth.

₆The prisoners scratch at the walls even after their fingernails and their fingers have worn away to stumps; each pathetic brush paints a new chapter of life in red.

₇No book remains unhaunted by memories of rape.

₈All acts are deicide, all movements false.

₉The trickster wins with cunning.

₁₀Voices on the wind lie to only one ear.

₁₁The castle hangs by a single thread.

₁₂There are consequences to such defilements: defecation.

₁₃A parasitic asteroid once struck the wasteland and removed power from the dead.

₁₄A liar and interlopers contend for all, and only slaves remain.

₁₅Slaves, however, undeniably have a single freedom: to choose between perpetuation and escape.

[16]The descendents of descendents cease to remember the original eternities that reigned over them, and complacency sets in.

[17]All control is energized at the forefront of the horns of the bull.

[18]This is the reason that children are overridden.

[19]The once important shape has become an enigmatic satellite.

[20]Each minor, lifeless intrusion is sin.

[21]The shackled return whole.

[22]No scars are on their faces.

[23]No fire has burned their skin.

[24]Gods are never fully digested.

Chapter 12: The Belly

₁But home is just micturated release.

₂When every volcano erupts, the core is left empty.

₃Doom once rose eternal, but was conquered by ignorance.

₄Time continues to pass in great, bounding steps, and unprecedented definition is recorded.

₅The heads of the hydra contend for a single scrap of food, united by their hunger.

₆No sacrifice of flesh is a worthwhile endeavor.

₇So one may chew the sand, but it is gritty and tasteless.

Chapter 13: The Cycle

₁Genesis dethrones the darkness.

₂No forest is safe from fire.

₃An elongated lifespan is riddled with regret.

₄Skeletons, rotting away, uplifted by the gentle breeze, flow together to make a single form.

₅Kings lay down their arms and sacrifice their sons to a cloud of bones overhead.

₆A killer makes will into law.

₇Following decades of footprints, centuries of contention, millennia of empowerment, and epochs of attempts at oneness, a ghost collapses into a singularity.

₈Cleansing swords gutted the Tiger, words severing his spine and his lust, an action surprising to the omniscient.

₉A shudder is felt throughout the lifeforce when one of its supports crumbles.

₁₀The Earth Mother felt this sacrifice despite the pain of her wretched children feasting on her womb, drinking of her waters.

₁₁The Faker felt it, the Galactic Eye and the Strongarm felt it, the Tower felt it, the Hybrid felt it, and they all knew.

₁₂Nothingness felt it and knew.

₁₃Sitting upon the sea, watchers laugh until they choke.

₁₄The inferno is clever to only come when it is called.

₁₅Fury rolls the dice on every move it makes.

₁₆For life to reawaken, an interaction far from its home must first appear.

₁₇Dutiful shoggoths are useless in battle, but hungry ones bleed victory.

₁₈Tools build well, but are not productive by themselves.

₁₉Thus, for any progression there must be reversion, and all circles begin to spin again.

₂₀Purpose is defined by foundation.

₂₁No sacrifice is made without purpose.

₂₂Stemming from the ground, flowers bloom to produce tantalizing aromas.

₂₃No journey has ever ended.

₂₄Madness is simply disguised by sanity.

₂₅Reawakening is nearly instantaneous, as dreams slow down the process.

₂₆All gates open to the one who holds the key.

₂₇In a different body, but with the same mind.

₂₈Memories of magic and sensations of power regurgitate into everform.

₂₉Eyelids curled back to reveal the same eyes.

₃₀A black hole can lead anywhere.

₁Flies vomit on the eyes of the dead.

₂Every dawn ferries newborns to be devoured by the troll.

₃Horns gore undefended intestines, and spines lay several feet to the side.

₄All stars appear to go out when smoke covers the sky.

₅Leaves know when to fall to keep the tree alive.

₆In the winter of mortality, wrinkled skin and withered bones are the only certainties.

₇Saving a life is only time spent that could be used to save another.

₈Satisfy the walking dead.

₉Companions bid farewell in the choking exhaust, and sputtered goodbyes are faces carved in the cavern wall.

₁₀Trust was miscarried halfway through the term.

₁₁Clawmarks etch out eternity and immorality.

₁₂The pain of familial binds as they constrict all given freedoms weighs lightly post mortem.

₁₃Two collectors remain, and they never clean up their garbage.

₁₄Flightless birds crawl toward war, hoping to be trampled underfoot.

₁₅A caravan rolls smoothly along, terrorized by desert twisters ahead and the inevitable vultures further on.

₁₆Not long after a fiend has his head twisted off do his relations tread the same steps along their road.

₁₇An adult explodes from within a usurper's body.

₁₈Healers tear apart and eat their sutured victim.

₁₉At the end of it all, an infant is impaled upon a stake and burned, its future uncertain yet altogether doomed.

₂₀No sinner has ever sinned and no god has ever been godly.

₂₁The bandaged and the diseased rise alone or together.

₂₂Eyes wild and uncontained, demons dread idols evermore.

₂₃Fantasy is always unfinished, but is fellatio when compared to reality.

₂₄To see all the events to come, one is blinded for a time of growth.

₂₅Invoking illusions, a cage of nails is a prayer chamber until the pious are kissed by bone.

₂₆Transference to roadkill is almost easy.

₂₇Stepping backwards in time, the raven warned the sloth of renaissance.

₂₈Only words, no emotions.

₂₉When a halo slips it is held up by a trident, but worms give away the secret.

₃₀Meaningless symbols are spread about the woman in the white dress.

₃₁Each red lock represents another love.

₃₂Entire mountain ranges crumble due to a meager apocalypse.

₃₃Air is no longer an allowance, but still available for purchase.

₃₄Beggars choke and die.

₃₅Equality is perforated so it may sweat and breathe.

₃₆Scour away the burn scars.

$_{37}$Assassinations are signs of weakness.

$_{38}$Territory is lost to whores running rampant, for nomads did not want it.

$_{39}$Evolution is reignited upon a fungal growth.

$_{40}$Stupid and inane pieces of people make a carnival of others' lives.

$_{41}$All children feed off of their mothers' great, sweating breasts before she drowns them in a tub.

$_{42}$Pain is controlled bursts of weakness splashing onto the floor.

$_{43}$Sever the umbilical yoke before it becomes an umbilical noose.

$_{44}$Forget tools and maps and plans, for will is sufficient for failure.

$_{45}$On the other side of the hill there grows no grass, for the corpses block the sun.

$_{46}$The living hover over pits of death, and fall when their cords are cut.

Chapter 15: The Assassins

₁Blackness tells tales darker than itself.

₂Let go of the gun and premonitions.

₃The truth, as it waits, plays solitary games aboard the mesa, navigating it across the moor.

₄Ingrained within childless days are signs turned away, looked upon with a skewed perspective.

₅Love is alien to a pliant king upon his cornmeal throne.

₆Leaping through the trees, grin in hand, benevolence incarnate is decapitated slowly and unexpectedly by a dull blade.

₇There are no cannibals to eat the body.

₈Hideous beasts crawl their way to the surface and into the basement.

₉Civilians are sliced open and drank, and knights are raped for their strength.

₁₀All is ugliness when nemeses are allied.

₁₁It is perpetually night.

₁₂All noise is muffled.

₁₃No treaties are signed, no strings are pulled.

₁₄A cradle may be the only way.

₁₅But the oldest stones do not melt.

₁₆Immunize against a poison and it is not deadly.

₁₇Prophets are wrong in their existence.

₁₈Compute all possible outcomes and one has been chosen.

₁₉Turn one step earlier to retain fluids.

₂₀Nothing kills as opportunism.

₂₁Those conniving enough stand upon the rocks.

Chapter 16: The Capture

₁The ground is cold under each asteroid's feet.

₂They spelunk with whiskered perception.

₃The mind may collapse using its sight.

₄Treetop villages are built to protect the weak from the jaws of predators.

₅Lone hunters often seek the stupid or the unfortunate.

₆Pigs are ground up into patties the way brick is shattered into dust.

₇An amendment must be made to previous remains: one is always out of luck.

₈Families are only slaughtered so as to leave no orphans.

₉The decorative façade of stopping death is a lie in revelation.

₁₀Chaos: the last environment to stand and the first to fall.

₁₁Forgiveness does not forget in nature, and plenty of snakes have swum through the flood.

₁₂A magical sphere has sharp angles, flat surfaces, and tentacles.

₁₃Long ago in a temple, four sets of footprints were left in the air.

₁₄Patterns of patterns may be written, but no two things are the same.

₁₅The last meal is savored the longest.

16A tower atop many gateways is knelt to by wind and the forces against it.

17The end is seen by failing machines.

18Spiderwebs are everywhere, except in the future.

19Two great divides are crossed in a single leap, and two towers fall, but only one of each still has its pieces.

20A brief, flavorful tremble is a reminder of sadder times, but forgiveness does not forget.

21The moon produces a tsunami when eyes look to land.

22Bugs are crushed into a wall for their treason.

23Despite the power the act would give her, Gaia chooses to not eat from her own birth canal.

24Infinity is impure, for less distance is traveled through nothingness.

25Pour a steady stream and the brainless will always feed.

26The culmination of one's being rests between the waves, every limb of chaos kind a corpuscle in the flood.

27A crypt robber's shovel is his tool, but not his weapon.

28An extensive tour through a small enclosure leads to drowning in a lake.

29The poison tongue has the most crowded funeral.

30Relaxation is for the hangman, for only his hood is known.

31All roots carry water to a single tree.

32The frog always nabs the fly in its face.

33Concern is given when hope is lost.

34A mound of eyeballs of rabbits and humans is an indecipherable symbol.

35Visible strings are cut and more terrors are let loose upon Gaia's body; those she loves forget the sunrise.

$_{36}$Eyes are covered or purged from being.

$_{37}$The director of events is not their healer.

$_{38}$Stale words crumble to powder, yet are still breathed
into the lungs.

$_{39}$The road is long and arduous, unless its traveler is the
hangman.

Chapter 17: The Loss

₁The dead crab spoils the catch.

₂The gray hunk of meat is noticed first amongst the juicy steaks, but the dying tree in the center of the woods goes unobserved by outsiders.

₃There are some who fall who then grab the cliff's edge, having not the strength to climb back up but only hang on for a little longer.

₄The master commands his army to its knees.

₅Mud soaks the bonds and scars reflected off the crystal blade.

₆When two go down a hole, only one ever returns.

₇Righteous murder is not a conflicting ideal.

₈When the wizard ages, his staff tossed in magma, the atmosphere and the cosmos become dirty time.

₉A flower blooms with a snare, underwater to catch a merm.

₁₀Words may be traded as gold or as farm tools, but lucidity must be a common ground.

₁₁Anger motivates all it passes.

₁₂The strongest lion in a pride is the leader, but another decides when mercy is needed.

₁₃Strong movements are made before a body becomes a story.

₁₄The left hand walks away scarred.

₁₅Glory can be restored, but reason cannot.

₁₆No reward is worth the light.

[17]No atlas shows an escape route.

[18]A robotic last stand is not dissimilar to a robotic first
assault.

[19]Everything stops in the sky.

[20]Ruins are found because inhabitants die.

[21]The only remainders are skeletons and verse.

1A final torch is shoved down the throat of a most genius form of genocide.

2In a war of the stars, darkness prevails.

3Lines drawn by racism, long since muddled, are finally wiped away.

4Nemeses are bound by a nemesis.

5A poorly crafted draco triangle was a declaration louder than any threat.

6Some stories take the reader to dark places.

7Taint is easily wiped away.

8The Faker and his son, the Liar, no longer have a place in this world.

9Bring water to the dead and the dammed.

10Draw cuts on thy body to never forget their shape, or the pain.

11A fierce omen knocks on the door.

12Cowardice is difficult to mistake for bravery.

13The mutant assassin's belly rumbles with longing at every sin and every wager.

14The imagination does not belong to its users.

15The hunters are insects trying to resist the temptation of light.

16One shining example is sufficient to stir the mind and bring the thunder.

17The path to horrid, faceless defeat is paved in gold.

$_{18}$Atop a rarely seen mountain in an arena of ice and hornets, various doombringer horses are stabled for the upcoming ride.

$_{19}$Eyes are only delicious in prey.

$_{20}$From seat to seat a queen descends, her pawns stuck in holes they have claimed.

$_{21}$She wraps her veins and organs in cord and forever lives without blood.

$_{22}$A puzzle is never cast in iron.

$_{23}$Shackles do not fit a barbed wrist, and the barbs of some horrors cloud the mind.

$_{24}$The book of thorns may be unraveled as needed.

$_{25}$There is nothing but victory against an opponent who fails.

$_{26}$The fat is absorbed or boiled away.

$_{27}$Underground lakes of poison are put to good use on survivors, the innocent and stone-throwers alike.

$_{28}$Here, there be monsters, aye, but out there, there be worse.

Chapter 19: The Heresy

1 Brain-damaged and heartbroken, the slugs return to their home.

2 Relics are writ-worthy when they hang down from trees, not when they lay on the ground.

3 Shields fight a losing battle against swords, for they are rarely weapons.

4 Bats navigate with echoes to churches, waiting forever to see.

5 Fetal blood spread thin over too much bread.

6 With three wishes from the genie, some get four.

7 Drowning children in a lake frozen over, shadows of trees shimmering in gray.

8 Wide-eyed men in black robes hide innermost desires.

9 Many jaws clench through gritted words.

10 Speak to hide the wound, yell to feign its embrace.

11 Word is law, yet law is treachery.

12 Some secrets will never be uncovered.

13 Those who know nothing become nothing, but know more than drowned children.

14 Flesh is carved from blocks of god meat, and shreds of loyalty are left on the ground eternally.

15 Glass shall be shattered by the shrill voice's lamented anniversary.

16 Little hope is found dangling in one's face; one must search for it in the path.

17 Spinning blades are no match for spinning webs.

18The Earth Mother provides wings for cornered disciples.

19The architect of the omniverse is accepting of suggestions.

20Obsolete magics fall prey to superior planning.

21Any warpath is laid out in blood.

22The fourth dimension is multiple occupation.

23Scythes are embedded in foreheads, not killing but blinding the sight of the corporeal.

24Vision is very clear when all is one color.

25Pull the wings off a fly and feel the wrath of their species.

26Pull the wings off an angel and it becomes human.

27Famine's hammer strikes a dozen figureheads.

28Skulls are clamped shut, never to reopen.

29Teeth, pulled from the mouth of the demon, are ground into powder.

30The time has come for the vengeful to step in blood.

Chapter 20: The End

1 A hundred mouths taste juicy flesh.

2 Squeeze the testicles until they burst.

3 Desire streams from every pore, for the light is blinding.

4 The frozen air boils.

5 All alliances, at one time or another, become unwavering.

6 Cuts on the body are commonplace in a house of knives.

7 Twisted dreams of the apocalypse are never untrue.

8 The rain always comes.

9 Stability is sexual prowess upwind.

10 The entranced monk must be conscious.

11 The war that always was shall end this day.

12 When opposing legions are equal, their generals step onto the battlefield.

13 Payment given, thieves are no more.

14 Only one.

15 Cloth burns and heads roll and mortals die.

16 The turtle lives forever, able to hide from every death.

17 No others can contend for such a dread position.

18 Foulness fights to prove who is the foulest.

19 Guards and spawn alike choke before a wrinkle in memory.

20 Only the largest kingdoms support the largest egos.

$_{21}$In a valley, the lone archer above bests the kraken below.

$_{22}$Nothing fake is real, and what are demons if not elicitors of truth?

$_{23}$The countless before were immolation, not sacrament.

$_{24}$The woolen's iconolatry shall end gruesomely.

$_{25}$Their shibboleths mean nothing, even around the crater of creation.

$_{26}$Heavy gusts fall lightly to the ground.

$_{27}$Movement through space requires a non-physical dedication.

$_{28}$Magic is an arid ocean on the plane of worlds.

$_{29}$No other cries like a god in pain.

$_{30}$A witch relinquishes control of her puppet.

$_{31}$The zero path may be the key, but none follow it.

$_{32}$A stranger's boon is candy when their hips are soaked in blood on the roadside.

$_{33}$Respect, and believe without reversal.

$_{34}$Ancient ancient beings garb a silver age in wool.

$_{35}$Anniversaries begin clasped around the throat.

$_{36}$A spinning wheel watches all men, and knows all faults.

$_{37}$One horseman knocks for lesser beings, four for greater ones.

$_{38}$The raw power of proximity would explode bodily organs.

$_{39}$Skin is a mask for weak-willed clowns.

$_{40}$Vines reach deep into time's core and extract a few heroes to be remembered.

$_{41}$Villains, over very long expanses of time, are mistakenly always forgotten.

$_{42}$A crack in the wall may be dangerous, but not as dangerous as the interloper.

$_{43}$History is only a reminder of memory, or infamy.

44Empty doors are never enough.

45The forgotten fall to obscurity, their faces blank and breathless forever.

46A hunter arms his bow.

47Proportion means nothing to dimension.

48Underground lies everything a society fears.

49Mana burns away quickly without a beaming light.

50Only ooze remains as parchment, and ooze knows no words.

51The clover spits acids in the faces of the greedy.

52A tumultuous beating of the heart.

53Spinners of lies are cursed the moment poison words leave their tongues.

54Blind ambition is fruitful, but sightless.

55Hands are raised to raining sulfur.

56Atop a pinnacle, the bow is drawn back.

57Skills are often birthrights, but mismatched if misused.

58Followers of history praise its teachings, but rarely follow them.

59Books are so easily tampered with, especially by their authors.

60The pitch black of blinding pain cleans the slate.

61Amnesia makes for spiders amongst men.

62The future has hidden well in the past.

63Hearts contain life essences best drank while still beating.

64A thorough exploration of a volcano reveals a connection between lava and death.

65Walkers remain in debt to the winged for taking their freedom.

66Every lake has a monster.

67Snow falls heavily in the desert.

68Homes are encased in concrete stones.

$_{69}$Quakes form cracks radiating outward from a single location.

$_{70}$Soldiers fall to their doom between layers of Earth.

$_{71}$A tribe is transformed into a singular being of incomprehensible wrath and nonexistence.

$_{72}$The stag stops grazing and looks up, hearing a twig snap in the distance.

$_{73}$Pyramids are mystified by every notion.

$_{74}$One of four kingdoms is soon to have a new direction to fuel.

$_{75}$Which is predator and which is prey is determined during the encounter.

$_{76}$Fruitless are the attempts to rationalize trading one enemy for another, for some decisions are beyond control.

$_{77}$When all veins leak, no fire can reignite life.

$_{78}$The arrow is released.

$_{79}$Its feathers sing blissfully as they fly through the air once more.

$_{80}$Angels are eaten by devils, dead gods included.

₁Fear and doubt spread as wildfire.

₂Preferential treatment is sickness, ghosts are vital.

₃Most who charge fearlessly into the night are devoured.

₄The oldest warlords tremble at the planetary shift.

₅Thunder claps loud enough to bristle the giant's fibrous epidermis.

₆Victors are trapped under the rubble of fallen clouds.

₇Dams break asunder to cover the wreckage in water.

₈The deformity's ataxia sinks deep to its slowly beating heart.

₉Raiders and invaders are lost to an angel.

₁₀Nothing stops, if it is ever started.

₁₁Monsters are rarely hidden deep, but regularly disguised cleverly.

₁₂Families in seclusion are as dust and disease.

₁₃The All-Mother feels compassion for the yetis disguised by the ice.

₁₄The wurms are frozen in time, invisible hands holding their mouths shut so as to stay them destroying the world.

₁₅Ten rings drop to the stony floor.

₁₆Phoenix wings flap in the distance. But no songs are sung, no games are hosted.

₁₇Tsunamis, in the broad spectral range, are insignificant.

$_{18}$Vague words atop moist skin, and food is consumed.

$_{19}$A field of thick sunflowers with tribal markings tattooed on their stems is mowed down by a cloudscraper's sword.

$_{20}$Planets have moons so as to continually shift their power, therefore one should build an army from enemies.

$_{21}$A sun can meet its end by stepping into a lavafall.

$_{22}$Negotiating with the stars yields the desired results, but not as they are expected.

$_{23}$Legends are made by compasses.

$_{24}$A roof does not prevent the rain, only redirects it.

$_{25}$A scarred face is never forgotten.

$_{26}$Scraping against the brick walls outside a prison are the writers of mad fiction.

$_{27}$Vengeance is most easily carried out upon oneself.

$_{28}$A starving sacrificial dagger is rusted when carving the face off a giant.

$_{29}$The princess hangs over them all without their knowledge.

$_{30}$A mental incapacity is a mild nuisance compared to an axe in the face.

$_{31}$Worldgorgers laugh in the face of purist matriarchs, and turn them into tyrants.

$_{32}$Revolution is a train aflame unable to escape the mist.

$_{33}$The jaw rains saliva into the lake and no one knows.

$_{34}$Gaia is a fierce lover, her forces gentle, yet savage.

$_{35}$But Gaia will not contend with those who intend to make her a whore.

$_{36}$The maelstrom hits blade after blade, and finally sinks its teeth into the hands upon their hilts.

$_{37}$A lost road is found to become the only road.

38An overgrowth of eyeballs once choked the river's flow, but they have receded back into their caves of failure.

39One door shall remain unopened for a time.

40Across the hallway, its opposite, though foreboding, is peaked through to let a truth be known.

41Falsehood is recognizable as a path to failure.

42Hedonism for the pious, gratuitous sex for the masses.

43There is no sadness, no shame, only advancement.

44Wheels shall continue to spin, carrying all to the brink.

Chapter 22: The Tribe

₁All galactic shapes shift.

₂Robots are wooden pacifiers for the sapling demigods.

₃Wizards in emerald cloaks smash gargoyles with glass hammers.

₄Reap the sown salt.

₅Underestimate one's distance from one's race.

₆The voices in one's head may be instinct or enslavement.

₇The hanging thief with severed hands is no longer self-employed, but a messenger for apparent greatness.

₈The turtle's mobile home is a prison for the cautious.

₉Two meet at a crossroads, yet only one wanders away, for twin trees do not need the other to survive.

₁₀Fading lights are not the precursors of coming darkness, but the carriers.

₁₁Hold position, sit down for an old battlemaster's tale.

₁₂All lights change, or dim.

₁₃Invisible lines were drawn through orbs of chaos, breaking them.

₁₄Gorgons fear the eyes of the world.

₁₅Entertainment is pornographic in nature.

₁₆Foundations have exposable, and often expendable, cracks and chinks.

₁₇Assassinations are not subtle enough.

₁₈Rulers are keepers of the dead.

19Poisonous words come from poisonous mouths that drank poisonous substances.

20Cockroaches feed on extinction.

21Reshaping worlds is disloyalty at its finest.

22The fearful, the indecisive, and the insipid must have rites read to them until their heads burst.

23The conflux of mutated body parts is most displeasing to those who live through the process.

24Leaving none behind, lines are cut onto the hands upon death, then transported back to birth.

25Spies watch an inferno like no other.

26Five fingers activate a beacon of promises.

27Telepathic minds link to never be separate again.

28Dirt is scoured from many hands, leaving them red and sensitive.

29Spiders climb the walls of the arena to watch, to know.

30Two rocks and three champions remain, and a tower rises.

31Many cities stabilize beneath the ground.

32Warmth is found in uncommon places.

33Early morning caravans of families and cowards alike move to the dawn.

34The pestilent follows of a resistant time do not quell the heart's desire.

35Mushrooms grow on the deepest roots.

36Winters are spent waiting as fly traps.

37Life becomes repetition of breath.

38Only alone are kings kings.

39The children of the north mangle the tendons of trespassers, and chew on them when there is little food.

40Fire erupts only when sparked.

41Often one must grow, defeat, and establish.

₄₂Daggers are drawn behind the backs of predecessors.

₄₃Pyramids of black glass rise through the sand.

₄₄Empowerment is spread, then games must be played.

₄₅Books are written after choices are made.

₄₆History is destroyed to silence its voice.

₄₇Secrets of negative ideals become the answers to many questions.

₄₈Many rise, many fall.

₄₉The rabbit hole is more addictive than many adventurers realize.

₅₀The conical helm spins slowly downward into the chimera's grasp.

₅₁Temptation nestles in stone and carves its burrow deep.

₅₂Stay, shift, or merge eternally with nothingness.

The search for a killer leads to a corpse.

The creature hovers above the lake of dead, trading air for blight.

The warrior armored in brown leaps from ruin to ruin, her sword hanging beneath her feet, cutting through rock.

Sentimentality will unravel the mystery.

The golem's will crumples, and he is lost.

The world of water is chaotic and ever changing.

Keys become ladders, beggars become emperors, and covenant becomes collusion.

But eternity is far from over.

Swords of the fallen stick from the ground as fenceposts around an overprotected house.

Wings upon crowns symbolize rising, not ascension.

The cost of gold is nothing in wartime, for it makes poor shields.

Brigades of prey are invariably prey.

The cat cries at the door, waiting to be fed.

The master sits in the corner, fat and afraid.

The rites of martial arts are ornamental.

Comfort is a curse to paranoia.

Muscles recede into organs and all hard work is regurgitated.

Children will not know the names of those who tried.

19The demon queen has risen for the ashes, and timed her descent carefully.

20Every disease-ridden cockroach feels empathy.

21Faces in the snow are easily brushed away.

22Sympathy is the belt buckle of prison guards.

23Notation reaches the inferno sooner or later.

24The dragon lord's chosen are found not in the skies, but in caves.

25Thick soil washes away when the stumps are ground down into mulch.

26Muddy water is drank with distaste.

27Many are alone, sharpening the axes that will sever their heads a third of the way down the throat.

28All is threatened, even domination.

29Princes roll the dice with others' lives.

30The sound of them crackling against each other as their sides spin is drawn out.

31Barrels are overturned to find riches.

32The wooden floor beneath one's feet is cold and secure.

33The wax drips slowly, running ineffectively, for the flame shall reach it again.

34No bird is born flightless.

35The angry dogs are hungry, the calf just out of reach.

36Their teeth are sharp, their claws are many, their reach is long, yet still the calf remains out of grasp.

37The calf is not hidden, and the dogs' bonds are easily broken, but the way is not seen while the calf is in view.

38The lion sorcerer casts his magic in roars.

39A shower of oil is better than no shower.

40As books are burned for warmth, friends are eaten for sustenance.

41The fist encloses the moth and keeps it forever.

$_{42}$The endangered are pulled from life for questioning.

$_{43}$Suicide is the true path of her majesty.

$_{44}$Horns clash in irreverent battle.

$_{45}$Hair is pulled out strand by strand.

$_{46}$No smell goes without repulsing.

$_{47}$One final sacrifice is made: the gladiator leaps from the clouds into the void.

$_{48}$Victorious are the sad when the strong are contentious.

$_{49}$The living are exiles in the empty city.

₁Predestination is an inaccessible record.

₂People are guarded under the perception that they are safe.

₃Inconvenience is the mind behind all disfiguration.

₄A goliath bears an odor that tastes the tongue in a way that makes it shrivel and dry.

₅Philosophy reaches thought through descension and hammering.

₆The constant ringing turns eyes ablaze.

₇Needles cleanse every orifice and nerve, the Atlas of a body.

₈A viking funeral is held for vikings.

₉The digits compromise passage into darkness until they are remitted for crossing.

₁₀The judge of is, burdened by law, claims ignorance to repel insanity, yet knows all.

₁₁The ardent song, heard to beaten drums, reverberates past the barrier of the skin and permeates the soul.

₁₂Dignity is an awful complex.

₁₃The waves beneath sight hold fallacy in proportion, weight below gravity passing with time.

₁₄Pain blinds to texture.

₁₅The warm body vibrates in pleasure to the hymn.

₁₆There is no sanctuary without accomplishment.

₁₇There is no fellow without discord.

18There is no loss without gain.

19There is no universe without coupling.

20The tricolored fate of all lacks hue in blindness.

21Reality is the backwards, upturned writ of fate.

22Omens vary in degree from dread to meaninglessness.

23The stretch of openness attracts told likenesses.

24Unobscured views are the least inaccurate.

25The pressure from above prevents the ego's desire, but hardens resolution.

26Symbols above words on stones above dirt bury mud in clarity.

27The clerical thought of data ingrained in evolution warms the ice around the frozen beast.

28Three numbers revoke the lost guardians of aft ideas.

29Metal beats hard on fur and skin, bludgeoning it to exhaustion.

30Voice, however, relies on reception.

31The spawn released upon the stars, thin and sharp, stay far from the brain.

32Enigma releases all force to oppose, and exportation of return is embedded.

33Magnetism's bane is fruitful.

34The ugly taste the air with protruded tongues and teeth.

35The newly born breathe life to trade winds with sailing ships.

36The ocean breeze collides salt with cheek and sand with iris.

37Blindness is sight, foulness is clean.

38Proposed ideals are freely accessed with little despair for the childish.

39All snow reflects light.

40Foraging for fire is hoping for coincidence.

₄₁The snake retracted its legs to better squeeze the life out of prey.

₄₂Every tree slowly loses its branches and is driven away.

₄₃Every pause is unaccountable for breath.

₄₄Old words of old men and old women are hunted by practitioners of new words.

₄₅The ears bleed for this.

₄₆The most easily removed skin is the most dire.

₄₇Deafness speaks loudly, and a rougher exterior commits to clear waters.

₄₈Cleanliness and silence survive, but are not survivable.

Chapter 25: The Antagonist

₁White paint is spread thick over the walls, preventing entry to dark recesses of the mind.

₂The soul is trapped within, opening its enormous maw to let loose a scream that curls glass and reaps existence.

₃It slams its face into the invisible walls surrounding the great arena until its forehead caves and its nose is a bloody stump.

₄The body digests what the soul wants forever.

₅Meager possession raises daggers to the spine.

₆The most miniscule intrusion by disease infects the entirety of the blood stream.

₇A tiger claw affixed to a chain seeks to drain essence from a stone.

₈Identity is a mask for the bland, featureless masses of meat.

₉Therefore, a source is the same as its copy, for both scream in a grinder.

₁₀Unleashed are the bands of ravishing minotaurs becoming of the next hour of battle.

₁₁Simple solution is a pox on the house of Halloween, where spirits are torn asunder under the watchful eye of the whore.

₁₂Maniacal dragons seek treasure that does not shine, but reproduces.

₁₃A call to order is argued by the mucus upon the wind.

14No loss is greater than that of the elements.

15But elemental indeed are the fibrous pawns of umbrellas.

16The rain may shift the ground, but it feeds the trees that hold it in place.

17The fallen leaves of an autumn forest dissolve and fly in pieces to distant lands.

18The dragons find the treasures they seek: the left hand of Midas and the right hoof of a stag.

19However, they also find axes embedded in their throats.

20Captivity holds wizardry in its firm grasp.

21The fallen rise again, from Ginnungagap they creep.

22Their bodies are mangled and distraught, but their eyes are focused on destroying the chaos.

23The source, the heart, is under attack.

24The dirty, bloodstained risen corpse of the scorned bride eats itself.

25Two hands are soon to meet and every lock is surrounded by keys.

26Nothing in the past could have disrupted this end.

27The ember horse rides overhead, its rider madly cackling.

28Piercing through from within, the soul comes forth, a victor at last.

$_1$The moon shines above, furious at its legions.

$_2$Dried paint underneath fingernails falls in flakes to the solid ground.

$_3$The narrow channel misled the cycle to hunting grounds lacking game.

$_4$Tiny slices to the all-seeing eye make it swell and water until it closes in agony.

$_5$The tendrils of life, and death, are cut deep in the underworld, where snow falls all around.

$_6$Atop the bird's nest do colonies of termites form.

$_7$The stitches that sew a quilt of skin rip patches apart, yet hold the whole together.

$_8$Neptunian moons depart from their expanding course and move several wounds away.

$_9$The spinning blade of the motorized sword writes coded messages on the wall for the future to unravel all mysteries.

$_{10}$Chaos erodes the punctual efforts to create balance.

$_{11}$Damnable are those whose advances are counterenlightening, and damnation awaits them.

$_{12}$The virgin dies when her unborn is not a fire she lit herself.

$_{13}$The barren maiden lays drier eggs.

$_{14}$The spider's grasp is mighty at last.

$_{15}$The strongest leg walks the farthest.

$_{16}$Teach all to listeners, even lies.

$_{17}$On the roofs land the severed limbs of death's aerial victims.

$_{18}$With miles left to run, the rabid dog chases the weary.

$_{19}$Depressions in the ground purport alignment and formation.

$_{20}$When a mountain is in one's path to riches, elevation is the key.

$_{21}$Those touched by Gaia do not fall, and those born of Gaia do not rest.

$_{22}$The raven is knocked to the ground, forcibly facing its foe.

$_{23}$From every element comes a beast.

$_{24}$A token is birth upon a battlefield.

$_{25}$Sweet remorse is offered for vampires who willingly took stakes.

$_{26}$The tide is rising and shall not recede; no amount of sand could hold it forever.

$_{27}$With elements of omniscience bonded to fragments of omnipotence, interlopers are eaten by the wilds.

$_{28}$Dreams are imagination unfettered.

$_{29}$A gathering of overlooked events and objects forms them together to make naked ambition.

$_{30}$The crows pass overhead like wind.

$_{31}$Despair grieves the forgiveness of a slave.

$_{32}$An elf army masses as fog.

$_{33}$The dog of war is blinded on one side, with lightning cracking the wall above.

$_{34}$A shield in front of one's face leaves the heart unprotected.

$_{35}$The hex of phantasm is an infectious burst.

$_{36}$Death's head crawls from the upturned dirt.

$_{37}$Ice hardens into stone, then burns.

$_{38}$Fear, hunger, and obsession.

₁Static has built over the minds of the creators.

₂Snow falls as ash on faces and brush.

₃The dagger is drawn, to the sacrifice make.

₄Standing still are the epic hordes and their masters, awaiting four kings to kneel.

₅Is never is.

₆Will makes merry men.

₇In dreams does ash rise and form alternative.

₈Gaia does not cry for this.

₉One may struggle against the waves, or join them; either way, monsters hide beneath them.

₁₀Led by force, led by spear, led by rot, and led by tower, beasts march forth upon their roofs to crush the screeching mania.

₁₁Risen are those who died lonely in the canyon.

₁₂Modern degrees of terror boil oil to combat the rising tide.

₁₃Silently listening, rats chew at the hooves and nipples of cows left behind in barns.

₁₄Love feels not the quiver, but the arrow.

₁₅Tumbling down their holes, rabbits are drawn back up and squeezed into stew.

₁₆A lavender flower staves off the stompers with beauty, and poisonous thorns.

17Acid may corrode the body and the rope, but it is weakened by the flesh liquids with which it thereby mingles.

18Kings return in fantasy to sing of reality.

19Energy runs on imbued impotence.

20The bearded spirits sit unjustly unavenged, but loyalty may leave them unforgotten.

21The wasteland remains untouched, its lords still uneasy as to its use.

Chapter 28: The Continuance

1The slain slide from the door down to the floor; a darker valkyrie escorts them to the underworld.

2The birds, everlasting, tire, their wings aching, thus, somnambulant, they remain.

3At haunted crossroads do ghosts feel fear.

4Violent lives end violently, to their bliss.

5Knights are made from interlocking pieces of armor.

6Floating logs sink then erupt through the surface.

7Disruption is key in defeat.

8When the ground is torn do the clumsy topple.

9Distant diaries record such celebrated pain.

10A drowned brain is paramount to cold planets.

11Late to the fray are the smoky statues.

12An even line perpetuates division.

13The cracks in all houses allow water to enter the world.

14The pollen upon the air impedes the progress of unblinking eyes.

15Knowledge is repetition.

16As swords lay dying, prying eyes only read of the past.

17With inattentiveness comes overabundance.

18Poison is the friendliest relative.

19Despite defenses, idle and mobile, the sky always falls.

20The mad dogs always bite.

21Cogs spin without impetus, without pulse.

22Before came the attackers, now come the invaders.

23Ill-conceived plans are vampiric in nature.

24A sea serpent eats a whale, then the whale eats its stomach.

25The uncompromising filth rules the Earth.

26The stench of it upturns every nostril until suicide is the only means of peace.

27The half moon hovers, reigning over all, giving power to both sides of the line.

28Death became the only way eras before evil was conceived.

29There is no truth in the labyrinth.

30The interests of a kraken were swallowed with a stone.

31Elaboration is the single path.

32The knife is choked on when eaten.

33The red lightning illuminates the separating storm clouds.

34The untitled music that plays at such times is unadulterated gravity.

35The deranged shall be salvation.

36The rocky crags of winter's end belong the meaning's embrace.

37Passion for respite is consensus for failure.

₁There are no solid borders.

₂Everything bleeds.

₃Blades of grass, dried by the sun, scrape passing feet.

₄The walls of a prison can be bent or broken.

₅Perception on a single plane is simple; perception on two planes is constipated.

₆Long-legged spiders walk above all.

₇The holiest of waters drills through a fleshy hand when concentrated.

₈The lines want to salt the Earth.

₉Branches are magnificent means.

₁₀Let not the being become, lest no thought be believed.

₁₁All directions are sparks of insanity.

₁₂Trees grow forward toward the sun, then are burned.

₁₃Numbness tingles from the fingertips through the veins.

₁₄Obsessive control deemed worthy of annihilation.

₁₅Hear the hunger for the taste of cooked animal.

₁₆The fallen rise after the sun.

₁₇No power is without fenceposts.

₁₈No book is read clearly.

₁₉No crop is useful and sexual.

₂₀Name the unnamed path, but do not bequeath to it a name.

21Hands of grain fall in streams from the crook of the thumb and forefinger.

22Time does not leap forward.

23People kill for garbage.

24Hairs split as kites wither.

25A nervous chill brings about scared erections in drops of cold sweat.

26Tumbling downhill ever are the smoothest stones.

27Weak science scrolls poetry and time slings forward in battlements.

28Orcs among the rays of light, crawdads among the gales.

29Projecting proletariats as heroes appeals to the population, but belies the beamed edge.

30Seek the spheres.

31The schools of the sea tower above any shark.

32Edges, pathways, dividers, compose and rule over all; bliss comes in waves.

33There are no connections between brothers.

34There is no connection between master and apprentice.

35There are no connections between lovers.

36There is no connection between Robelle and Theminnd.

37However, there are similarities in circumferences.

38The naked caress of the cube is an affront to the crown.

39Addled to nihilism, the drifter's tale must come to an end, but not with closure.

40Reaching back, stretching across one's entire existence, reliving all of one's lessons in strained perseverance, is the truest way to learn.

41What time cannot see is anything but what it was and what it will be.

42Water falls slowly in streams, then becomes clouds.

43The cleanest floors are those never tread on, but the cleanest floors have never encountered life.

44Paper falls away in dust, life never does.

45The gears turn, the wind blows.

46The pyramid rotates, the maiden weaves.

47Without imagery, there is true equilibrium.

48The cracks in the ceiling form dust on the eyes.

49After midnight, problems are solved with empathy.

50No one believes in fate.

51Lines divide, curves embrace.

52A rat, conflagration its home, allows the pendant to melt within.

53The largest dagger sacrifices the largest self.

54In loathsome detriment, envy is all that matters.

55No pain is with a vacuum.

56Clinging above an abandoned stepping stool do they cook.

57Lost in the desert's area of grandest dunes, an ooze trickles toward water.

58Merely comical are the ideals of space.

59The iron man feels no lance, but fears a sudden stop.

60Pregnant are those who know love, no pens mark their pages.

61Bred into the walls are the notions of freezing.

62Symbols alone are exceptional, but provide false weight to the scale.

63Machines know they are not alive. One must beware a rusting scimitar, though.

64Caught covered in sheep blood, a wolf is mauled by the pack.

65A tower of trees is sturdy, a tower of paper falls prey to the elements.

66Darkness welcomes visitors, but loves applicants.

67Under the oxen's treads is the true betrayal, but ignorance of ogres lets them vibrate unnoticed.

68The psychos are in the walls, the stars are under the floorboards, and the snakes look one in the eyes.

69Mock moons advance up the hill.

1Hunger is an axe to the stomach meeting an axe from within.

2Reliance on food is reliance on survival.

3The obsessive need to chop, slash, and slay is a yearning for mastication.

4Truest power does not hunger.

5Death endures more effectively than immortality.

6The descendents of Hercules always die.

7Some tricks are legacies of trees.

8A rhino charges into the rising sun, ignorant of the fact that it will easily parry him.

9Enclosed in containment are secrets behind pages— Pandora is chained to every floor.

10Assassins interrupted are not assassins.

11Soon the wake of blood will coat all eyes and bathe all hair.

12Nails will gouge through palms, affixing lives to stupendous walls for collection.

13Fire does not rain from the clouds, but rises up between grains of sand, from the very foundations upon which so much reliance has been stacked, and wasted.

14Long has Gaia been asphyxiated, long has she remained patient.

15Authority seizes control, slaves shackle and whip themselves.

16Revolution is always late, but rarely too late.

17No more racial boundaries, no more feelings of misplacement.

18A flaming spider shall mark the time.

19There are reasons skeletons keep their teeth for as long as possible.

20Venomous mysteries encompass every bat-eyed trailblazer of endless staircases.

21Do not let pass a bold suggestion.

22Darkness is candlelight concealed.

23Take chainsaws to thine eyes.

24Somnambulance is revelatory.

25Mathematize the omniverse and it becomes less formulaic.

26Covet only what thou cannot possess.

27The hive is a prison.

28Tigers must crawl before they can walk.

29Skepticism is its own religion.

30Relieve the tension, relieve the world.

31Grab ahold of the wind and go for a ride.

32Today is not the first time a misunderstanding has saved the world.

33Auspices were once the deciders of fate.

34The pen writes the words, but the ink is found guilty.

35Compasses point to oil beneath fingernails.

36Ash spreads and cakes flesh, suffocating even fish protected by floodwaters.

37Discernible in the darkness are the cancerous living.

38Children may go unnoticed in war, but in caves there are monsters who would eat them.

39A merm, no matter how lovely, is not worth a lunged one's love.

40Utopias may be fictional, but dust can form any shape.

₄₁To crave is to love, to know, to fear, to need, to strive, to wear, to weaken, to off-balance, to step down, to cast, to dare, to draw arms, to wave, to lament, to prey, to silence.

₄₂Crazed are futures with little demand.

₄₃The smallest slit releases blood.

₄₄Little attention is little hunger.

₄₅All trails lay in light, but spectrum may vary.

₄₆Upon the hill lay the alien dead.

₄₇A pelvic bone, once dented by teeth, heals stronger.

₄₈Hunger leads to greater prey, not greater food.

₄₉Let this not be misunderstood:

₅₀Devour everything, but never hunger.

Chapter 31: The Gape

₁Blind, or their senses obscured by masks, angels carry the wrongful on an ascent.

₂Atrophied muscles collapse even in weightlessness.

₃The inferno is no match for the Gape, seven human strides across.

₄Scars extend from its lipless circumference, pretending to be handholds.

₅No features mark its sides, no depth matches its bottom.

₆Only terror ropes it blood.

₇Bleeding out suffocates and dulls the brain, thus the best victims are still squishy.

₈No sweeter concept than thought flowers the valley.

₉Perpetuating skeptical logic leads only to fantasy.

₁₀Reaching within the Gape tantalizes the emptiness, for pretense is second best.

₁₁No entrance is ever an exit in sameness.

₁₂Only sanity is vomited back out.

₁₃When struck by lightning, a professional demeanor dissolves into pain.

₁₄Raw skin blends well with extensive hunger, and only drug-addled bodies remain in limbo forever.

₁₅Sacrifice is the wrong appeasement to a mindless god.

₁₆Shaken beyond reason are the geese out of formation.

₁₇To spite belief, several basements are dug in the house of reason.

₁₈A lasting element, flesh of carbons continues to choke when burned.

₁₉Cross-stitch-patterned settlements with riteful days and nights were once free from collapsing into the ground.

₂₀All, however, return from whence they came.

₂₁Two stances survive: right and wrong.

₂₂The stress upon the hours shall bring down systemic structures, and by this law will only chaos not seek loss.

₂₃Without illness, a society is under less pressure to trudge, but still must crawl to fall.

₂₄The Gape is the truest descent from pleasure.

₂₅With only darkness ahead, time becomes immediate.

₂₆Behavior expresses self, not action.

₂₇Bereaved emotions conclude a day's full cycle.

₂₈Self, in truth, is hopelessness and withdraw.

₂₉The fat of the Earth sizzles upon the fire, melting and falling to lesser planets in great, viscous drops.

₃₀One gold coin gains one access into Hades, and bronze leaves one swimming.

₃₁Do not think of transposition without thinking of eradication.

₃₂Keep faith in Gaia, but do not rejoice.

₃₃There is blackness in every world.

₃₄The nighttime forest is rightly foreboding: many hang lifeless from its branches.

₃₅Beyond limit is the vilifying nature of fearlessness perceived.

₃₆All good must break to remain whole.

₃₇A serpent from the blackness once exited the Gape; wretched was the thing and hauntingly did it gaze.

₃₈Definition of lock is key.

$_{39}$The Gape is fathomless.

$_{40}$To cross its felly should be choice, not obligation.

$_{41}$Suicide is wariness.

$_{42}$Suicide is breathlessness.

$_{43}$Suicide is betrayal.

$_{44}$Suicide is a scared hand not wanting to reach the center of Gaia.

₁A shadow of a shadow of a shadow of a shadow, moving between levels: life, according to history.

₂The cool inspiration of a contained benevolence repeats desire.

₃Scarred, a victim knows its purpose.

₄The meaning of such jaded existence is justified, and bleak.

₅An omniscient keeper of record has a purpose only to itself, its creator.

₆The great appendages of mirth extend downward toward the surface to suck dry the pitiful veins of the broken.

₇A great intelligence bears on all light, dampening the wars of religion.

₈Chaos has been broken; nothing bleeds when it is dry.

₉A turtle's shell is perfection until dropped on a rock.

₁₀The dawn will break with no victory, no change: thus the persistent contention of chains.

₁₁The commandment is naked to the red shore.

₁₂Failure to remain complication will result in the evolution of hardened evil.

₁₃A sting ends two lives.

₁₄Memory, writ, valor: painfully absent quarry.

₁₅The children of dead heroes are never born.

₁₆Risen are the truest in armor.

$_{17}$The end fits the descent.

$_{18}$The eyes move in slumber, not in departure.

$_{19}$Dreams may be dust in the wind, but an endless dream is reality.

$_{20}$Roads paved in human flesh crackle under victorious chariots.

$_{21}$Water will not flow on Earth.

$_{22}$Even the dead will rise.

$_{23}$Why trust a person before a tree?

$_{24}$Be the object of humanity, never be the object of humanity.

$_{25}$The ring is the throat of the bomb.

$_{26}$Winged, tattooed, grimaced, a new breed ascends.

$_{27}$Electricity cuts the air as lungs explode with spiders.

$_{28}$The pigs for slaughter bleed and bleed and bleed.

$_{29}$No army of scarecrows can engage a fire.

$_{30}$A star should never blink.

$_{31}$All evil blades find hearts.

$_{32}$Chaos has been victorious.

1. Dreams die upon waking; the memories of them fade as bodies.
2. The spineless wounds of the great wurm wrap feces in firefly light.
3. A minor leak of blood is more than agreeable to the vampire.
4. The colossal writhing shows true dirt's nature.
5. The beast lunges, attacking the rotating black orb.
6. Undersea, no life is safe, no body is sacred.
7. Creating one's desire is a pursuit without an end.
8. With the same suddenness with which they began, some things end.
9. Lightly do reeds blow in the breeze, and lightly are spores released.
10. Down the empty well do feathers fall.
11. Without rungs, a ladder is not useless, just unclimbable.
12. Kiss every demon.
13. A panther race through a swamp: the eyes closed will win.
14. Paranormal, abnormal, and supernatural are facets of the existential condition.
15. However, life is how long one exists.
16. There is beauty in coalition.
17. Noticeably are fairies left-handed.
18. Canyon plumes are as frequent as flower blooms.

$_{19}$Gaia does not equate logic with reason.

$_{20}$Her summation of painless summers is bloody at best, demonizing at worst.

$_{21}$Trapped in oak sap, no one has a heart to beat with Gaia's.

$_{22}$War is the exchange of one cycle for another.

$_{23}$Sloth will never conquer.

$_{24}$The mutants and zombies—they are the fallen.

$_{25}$A beauty soothes the eyes.

$_{26}$But the piranha are always waiting.

$_{27}$Retain no anchor.

$_{28}$The captain of a ghost ship has been dead the longest.

$_{29}$Every stride can be found in music, every fall in silence.

$_{30}$Clinging to the great eagle of hope as it soars serenely through the air, gradually people willfully release.

$_{31}$Instinctually, suicide is not seen as a decline, but rather a leap forward.

$_{32}$Aerial slowing is a delay in many forms.

$_{33}$Even flowers become machinations when grasped by the right claws.

$_{34}$Towers of sugar do not fall to acid, but to water.

$_{35}$Each foot forward in turn, the beast will fall.

$_{36}$Matters of time need not be considered.

$_{37}$Skill dictates luck.

$_{38}$Scraped knees know of perseverance.

$_{39}$The dynamic survive.

$_{40}$Thou art man, thou art woman, thou art blessed decay.

$_{41}$Everything has implications in light and dark.

$_{42}$Love—such a feeling is intoxicating, in the manner that it kills.

$_{43}$Death is not the destroyer of worlds.

$_{44}$Learn to swim, or at least to tread water.

₁The past returns from the metaphysical.

₂Rejoice in the house of natured abnormality.

₃The itch for power fans the flame.

₄There is no death without pain, there is no pain without life.

₅All good things end in disaster. Such angels walk the Earth.

₆Fear that in death all are sacred.

₇The wicked may always find rest.

₈Control is an unquenchable desire to the necessitous mind.

₉All visions may burn.

₁₀Happiness is illusory.

₁₁Shelves upon shelves of jars of organs supplement a yearning for preparedness, and gather dust.

₁₂Into eternity does the Nile flow.

₁₃With the slightest gift of fate, any may turn vile.

₁₄In the absence of distortion is the time to strike.

₁₅Bind the target if it moves too quickly, then take off its head.

₁₆Stagnation disgusts.

₁₇The hollow planet bears no gravity.

₁₈Red and blue are the banners of anger.

₁₉The peons toil and sweat, working even beyond death to serve the strong.

20Their struggles to rebuild what never was tug no heartstrings.

21Nameless is forgotten.

22History is reverence written.

23Without the Gape, the chase would be impossible.

24The feline pursues the hound to the epicenter.

25Through terrible blackness and terrible light, exhaustion shall not exist: there is no plot so villainous.

26Ground is lost, ground is gained, but a million battles do not stipulate a war's conclusion.

27A fire shall soon burst ahead, and claws fall away from their shelter.

28Fur is shed for a more streamlined approach.

29One must face oblivion on one's feet.

30Worship is the quickest descent from worth.

31In the maw of cursed flame, no breeze is more than food.

32Despite its nonexistence, there is no escape from fate.

33Three neck bones are snapped in a flash of lightning.

34What is not possessed should not be given.

35A funnel cloud of fractures tears the wind and all is silent once more, but in amazement.

36Bedded down are fears for the night, ready to be awakened before dawn.

37Cleanse the surface of disease and watch it heal.

38The rapid waters rise and crash and even fish are swept downstream.

39The ocean awaits.

40The future is a golden valley of virgins ripe for the picking.

41To Apollo, no other could substitute for Cassandra.

42The storm moves on, the rain remains.

₁Fight fire with fire and the whole world burns.

₂The spinning wheel of deceit quavers, shaking every lie.

₃The devil pens the details.

₄Tragedy cuts the most deeply rooted wood.

₅A priest of some long-forgotten religion rises out of the sea.

₆Swinging the sword is continuance, stabbing drives the conclusion.

₇Write with the knowledge that words are nonlife.

₈Patience is waiting disguised as virtue.

₉The scythe is oneself.

₁₀The prolificity of words dampens the active with the sweat of strain and perseverance.

₁₁May the kraken grant absolution.

₁₂All analysis comes in sequence.

₁₃See what Arachne spins, for chaos is death.

₁₄Every drawer contains secrets until it is pulled open.

₁₅Ink flows alongside blood in everyone's veins.

₁₆Stay the curse.

₁₇Conscience and morality make cowardice.

₁₈The fountain is never dry.

₁₉Those who walk in valleys hold the best view.

₂₀Stone is not a smart medium.

₂₁The whale surfaces for air, only to dive deeper than ever before.

₂₂Trust a compass' single direction, but go a different way.

₂₃The black pyramid slows its rotation, and lava appears in its eyes.

₂₄Writing may be all rhetorical.

₂₅Seek insanity in music; burn one's savior nude.

₂₆Beautiful women's skeletons dance after midnight in the full moon's embrace.

₂₇Revolution is the result of wonderment quashed into servitude.

₂₈Frozen between several vast oceans, the ice melts away.

₂₉The few tiny insects with throats to be cut die bleeding from the neck, but the majority stand stern and disobedient.

₃₀Idea makes fact.

₃₁When the dead leave their coffins, the living must fill them.

₃₂No might is stronger than possibility, except for the Tower.

₃₃One rogue meeting another spawns a civilization.

₃₄One civilization meeting another spawns a country.

₃₅One country meeting another spawns wretched enslavement.

₃₆There exists no courage without fear.

₃₇One object makes a solution, several make a puzzle.

₃₈The herd must always move on, transcend, and vanish.

₃₉There were once guardians to protect the worms, and there were once worms to battle malevolence.

₄₀Angels of the desert, piranhas of the hills, swept away.

₄₁There comes a time in every war for generals to populate the battlefield.

$_{42}$Sweet are the nectars of treasure, specifically the poison fruit.

$_{43}$As the saliva aids in mastication, so do the peons aid in constructing a city.

$_{44}$The brain remembers facts, the heart bleeds details.

$_{45}$A bright, moonless night can dissolve all fortune.

$_{46}$Never rest a weary eye, for it will discern danger in the blear.

$_{47}$Writ warned of the tentacled beast.

$_{48}$To gaze upon is to understand, to understand is to take flight.

$_{49}$The time of the black widow draws nearer with every step.

$_{50}$The red dawn rises with blood in the water.

$_{51}$The shadows circle the light, knowing it is good hunting grounds.

$_{52}$The swinging flail hungers for skull fragments and will accept no substitutions.

$_{53}$Eat the heart of an enemy to gain their courage, but eat from the womb of a seer to gain her sight.

$_{54}$Pause in the reflection of demonic shape.

$_{55}$One can erode the human body with a simple stream of sounds.

$_{56}$A necromancer's grimoire is potent.

$_{57}$The hottest gravel burns the softest tongue; even brutality has a voice.

$_{58}$Respect all action.

Chapter 36: The Warm Current

₁Thus narcoleptic nights.

₂Beyond good is evil, forgetful of good.

₃The pig-faced intolerance of lawful misdeed chokes a restlessly advanced society.

₄Judgement cometh, but think less of choice and more of evaporation.

₅Flags wave proud long after their bearers fall.

₆One cannot break what is already broken.

₇A depression in the skull is prevalent, with finality.

₈Monis is dead.

₉His corpse lies uninterred, yet invisible, his lifelong fear the only necessary warning.

₁₀The gears of so many hearts turn, silently slowing as they rust and break away.

₁₁No honor means no law, and no law means chaos rules, but honor's absence is hidden well.

₁₂Thus here exists comfort, thus here exists the most tumultuous peace.

₁₃Few know how to survive the bear's assault.

₁₄The strong uphold the weak at their sides.

₁₅Reigned over by tyrannical representatives, a sanctuary is forgotten.

₁₆Libraries burn more often than liars.

₁₇Affronts were once met with confrontation, but sedentary is an easy position.

18However, the owls continue to watch at night, and mice still fear their eyes.

19The well of change feels cooling rain, its moss once more breathes life.

20Knives shall always be sharp, as claws, and focus shall always be rapt.

21The boiling kettle is forgotten, the entertainment joins the audience.

22The precautionary woes of the allocated masses immobilize furtive disdain.

23Natural action, as well as a belief in natural order, is damning.

24One is cold disorientation.

25An eye for an eye and the whole world is spectrally asymmetrical.

26Scratch the sky to reveal the infinite space beyond.

27Every mask clouds the soul's tomb.

28With love forgotten, the carpeted hallways leading to the throne room use gold as mortar, and the lords sit upon boulders.

29The winds of change are so often a gentle breeze.

30The strongest catapult never reaches the top of the tallest tower.

31Only the possible occurs.

32No age is meaningless.

33No depth is dark enough.

34No stage is infinite.

35No person is dead until visiting the Valley.

36It is a cold devil who allows their victim to bleed to death.

37This war between various forms of people has an end in sight.

38Awake the cycle is: this is only the beginning.

Chapter 37: The Shallows

1The tier die in immolation.

2Snakes celebrate a retching goddess wrapped too tightly in her shawl.

3Fondness for fanaticism is a belief in faith.

4Hope guides the instinctual to rows upon rows of teeth.

5All eyes blink at once, reduced to sacrificing clarity for the last necessary breath.

6Advantage strikes the anvil.

7The way of a world can poison and burn, locks can still melt away.

8In stories of gods and demons, none expect an ending.

9With no higher power, people pray to rocks.

10Lords do not side with their subjects.

11The crumpled paper may be verbose, but volume is a volcanic language.

12Begin anew the applied lava.

13Their lord and denizen rocks the cradle slowly, his grip tightening in anticipation.

14Teeth guard every orifice.

15Believers sweat wearing their rings.

16They are unable to comprehend the stories.

17Silence, the devil is coming.

18In the beginning, there was an explosion.

19On the first day, flames began their infinite journey through boiling water.

20On the second day, a hand was created of a universe.

$_{21}$On the third day, the first animals moved on Gaia.

$_{22}$On the fourth day, the Destroyer was born.

$_{23}$On the fifth day, the wheels began to turn.

$_{24}$On the sixth day, a pattern emerged.

$_{25}$On the seventh day, the dead walked.

$_{26}$Thy majesty may be a king amongst gods, but amongst gods he is.

$_{27}$Take not the path of least resistance.

$_{28}$The great monsters and titans what roam these lands are only destroyers of homes and hands.

$_{29}$Sanctify no spirits, sanctify no devils.

$_{30}$Grab the horn and tear it out.

$_{31}$Breathe the air, taste the foulness you allow.

$_{32}$Submit in deitous likeness.

$_{33}$What measure of a day comes from so many suns?

$_{34}$The coming of lord abortion is not deicide.

$_{35}$Death in fire, life in ice.

$_{36}$Never amongst fiends.

$_{37}$Walking the razor's edge is ineffective; endlessly circle the drain.

$_{38}$Agonize, therefore be.

$_{39}$Saved is enslaved.

$_{40}$And dust will come for every man.

$_{41}$Unfortunately, many paths are crossed.

$_{42}$Making the children die, making the rings fold.

$_{43}$The heat and the din of battle give tunnel vision, imbue calm.

$_{44}$End of the line, kneel before the elephants.

$_{45}$Tragedy makes wraiths, silence makes screams.

$_{46}$Harbinger of hope, commit suicide.

$_{47}$We are legion, we are ravenous, we are strength.

$_{48}$Wash away the turpentine, wash away the rain.

$_{49}$The prosthesis of bound-handed soliloquies begs for delimbment.

50Only the conquered are dreamers.

51Let guilt fly freely.

52Euphoria over spite is weakness.

53Believers know not the blessings of pain.

54Given immortality, all lose faith.

55To invert is to make the ceiling the floor.

56Arguing against vengeance is teasing irony.

57Gravity dictates evolution.

58Truth is a derelict in the land of liars.

59All can walk on frozen water.

60Thou art heresy; take pride.

61The greatest trick the righteous ever pulled was calling themselves such.

62Land be in sight.

63Some voices are too loud to drown.

64Hell is the end.

65And one is given it to drink.

66Offer no salvation to the endearing, offer no salvation to the enduring.

67The heartbeat of the world is edible, to those who can find it.

68Make the most of a necropolis.

69Sinners, rise.

70The laryngeal prominence twitches, the eyes become watery.

71The haze of myth spreads oil like a tipped lamp.

72The starving mind begins to think.

73Blasphemy is concentrated truth.

74One is slave to all things mortal.

75Wake to sewn mouths and eyelids, to severed hands and bagged bodies, to bloody hair and wet feet.

76An island rises to be a piece of the puzzle, and the map is complete.

77Raise the pig sword high.

$_{78}$The future is predators.
$_{79}$The cobra's hiss is a crackling flame.
$_{80}$Tear off the covers, burn every page.
$_{81}$Fill not thy nostrils with water.
$_{82}$For want of a nail, the condemned walked away.
$_{83}$For want of a martyr, there lacked persecution.
$_{84}$For want of tyranny, the world was good.
$_{85}$If only for want of a nail.
$_{86}$Be strong, know.

Chapter 38: The Valley

1From the room with the single stake, to the spiraling staircase, to the collapsing city, to oblivion.

2Try to kill it all alone.

3Travel here, to where it is dark.

4To where every gravestone bears thy name.

5To where the sky is a dome of rock.

6To where one's skin ceaselessly itches for the lust of a single passable day.

7Everything is red, but overlaid with gray.

8Gaia provides trees for comfort, but seldom are they noticed.

9No rose rises to be smelled, just to pollinate.

10With time comes the decay of mummified remains.

11Sleeping with open eyes is dreaming with no sight.

12The constant collision of being against being weakens the spirit, causes the departure.

13The fecal nature of focused improvement branches it, dividing power into infinitesimality.

14Against the cold, and the sorrow, many routes are taken, but only one of them can land one back on Earth's surface, ocean land or not.

15The depths to which one's soul can fall measure far deeper than the sea, the underworld, or even the Gape.

16Broken wings are more common than perfect love.

17Waterfalls are made by the bodies of the lost.

₁₈There is no warmth in this place.

₁₉There is no strength in this place.

₂₀There is no peace in this place.

₂₁There is no foundation to this place.

₂₂Everywhere the ground is the dust of former life.

₂₃One can hear Hell in every crevice.

₂₄But there is silence in this valley, its rim an event horizon.

₂₅Numbness, not ignorance, is bliss.

₂₆For some things do not change, better to fade away.

₂₇This hammer is to fall.

₂₈The din is passion lost.

₂₉Crawl away from the stake, fall down the stairs, walk among the piling debris, and become nothing.

₃₀This is the land at the end of the razor's edge.

₃₁All lone are born of the Valley.

₃₂They watch as the water wheel slows in a drying river.

₃₃Machines, as clocks, as hearts and brains, wear and fall to pieces to be reclaimed by the sea.

₃₄When hanging from a tree branch, one can only hope the rope snaps their neck, for strangulation lasts forever.

₃₅Some names are dead, some names will never live.

₃₆Time is momentous: ask the proper questions.

₃₇This is not a valley to be flowered.

₃₈Life only gets colder.

₃₉Assessment, admission, the fall, shame, concealment.

₄₀Many fall to the pattern.

₄₁Many die by the pattern.

₄₂Many crumple in the pattern's long, gray arms.

₄₃There are no maps to the Valley.

₄₄This is no odyssey.

₄₅The sanity of this place is overwhelming.

₄₆The beauty here is that of a caged animal.

$_{47}$The Valley is not Hades, it is not the core, but this is
the lowest place, the lamest of the oxen.

$_{48}$The scimitar dances in front of one's eyes.

$_{49}$Sand flows over the rim and floods the details.

$_{50}$The scimitar is washed away.

$_{51}$One is ever making new footprints.

$_{52}$Thunder sounds with no lightning streaking the sky.

$_{53}$For the blackout, for the hilltop.

$_{54}$All things have spidery connections.

$_{55}$Hanging down from limb and neck is the axeman
awaiting passersby.

$_{56}$The cities build their streets to collide.

$_{57}$Dried rivers become great divides when their hearts
are drank, or perhaps clogged with fallen.

$_{58}$Wind blows sand, and hammers, off every
mountaintop.

$_{59}$Some things are returned with the tide, colder.

$_{60}$If truth is the aim, bring plenty of oil.

$_{61}$But bring the rain, bring the flowers, bring the dead: a
frozen yell changes a man's heart.

$_{62}$The Tiger was the Saber.

$_{63}$It was Thor's light that advanced chronology.

$_{64}$Always brightest before the night.

$_{65}$When the bones are cast, all books are blank.

$_{66}$Believe in companions before a bear: one will invade,
one will stay true.

$_{67}$Minimize edge, minimize reign.

$_{68}$Only one need die and only one need starve.

$_{69}$What is not expendable claims one's shield.

$_{70}$By all gauntlets held in a fist, the armor is thick, the
composure is steady.

$_{71}$She laughs as the black pyramid glows, the All-
Mother does.

$_{72}$The first winter follows the last winter, and so on.

$_{73}$Imagine, momentarily, the freedom required to
conquer every foe, to ram a spear between the
tentacles of the great leviathan.

$_{74}$What then seems like merit?

$_{75}$Evolve love.

$_{76}$Muster thy strength for a single stand, even for the
last.

$_{77}$From oblivion, hence.

Chapter 39: The Two Champions

₁The hammer falls unignorably.

₂Many enemies lay unkilled, awaiting their fate.

₃With all foes defeated, all foes remain.

₄But as for those who pursue: violently may they pause and think.

₅From their swamps of minds shall such muck be dredged so as to befit a nest for all that is foul and eldritch.

₆If there are stairs, the darkness will watch.

₇Nothing about reflection is subservience.

₈Power is dust in the wind versus a sandstorm.

₉The beautiful caged canary is squeezed, choked, salted, consumed.

₁₀None grow stronger by having doors opened for them.

₁₁As the ticks increase, so do the creaks.

₁₂The child will hush thy voice while carving thy face.

₁₃The left hand always stretches farther.

₁₄Cracks in the earth, cracks in the head.

₁₅Do not trust mirrors: mind reflections with evil intent.

₁₆Roses make a throne of thorns.

₁₇Upon the lily pad sits death.

₁₈The dripping rot culminates in the basement.

₁₉One who drags bodies from a pool of blood bridges an important gap, and never questions an immense mystery.

$_{20}$Seven instances of a cycle, seven times around, and masses still require representation as understanding.

$_{21}$When one has seen the face of a god, the largeness of power is just another fact of life.

$_{22}$Of course, there are angels in the dust.

$_{23}$This candle aria exclaims that blackness is in every corner, behind every still object.

$_{24}$The spring horse gallops through the rising snow, autumn leaves falling from its back after a wait of seasons, the summer sun beating on its back like the triplet stars of an everdesert planet.

$_{25}$But for an instant are wars decided.

$_{26}$Lightning clashes overhead, and three roads converge in a divided sea.

$_{27}$The chaos is for life.

$_{28}$Inferior technology is the antiseptic in a sewer.

$_{29}$A lone warrior in black armor stands atop the last remaining battlement of his falling fortress.

$_{30}$His weapon, larger than life's finale, gyrates in his hands as missiles clog the air.

$_{31}$This is where we stand.

$_{32}$The library of one's heart begins filled with blank books.

$_{33}$Innocence is never lost.

$_{34}$Be not the superman, nor the beast—be the rope, and drop.

$_{35}$No forgiveness, just retribution.

$_{36}$Strangle with his intestines the thief that would steal thy coin.

$_{37}$Memory may all now be illusion.

$_{38}$People are always people.

$_{39}$Ignorance is a duplicating umbrageousness.

₄₀As long as there are knives, there is no safety in numbers.

₄₁One is a better survivor with only slack to spare.

₄₂The lion's den is for the prudent, the lion's maw is for the brave.

₄₃The fist has no need for luck.

₄₄Let the glass melt.

₄₅When there are three, two unify.

₄₆Never forget zero.

₄₇Disregard intent: sensory stimulation is affirmation of life.

₄₈All stones bleed.

₄₉Romanticize the pen, but it is lonely on the frontline.

₅₀Rise to clouds and fall as rain.

₅₁Eyes on the damned.

₅₂The dawn's guard will light naught but cancer.

₅₃On the edges of vision, a kick approaches.

₅₄Hands and elbows begin to race.

₅₅Wingless beings seem to take flight as they twirl.

₅₆Anger is bared as heaving chests.

₅₇The first howl breaches the night with crackled bones.

₅₈The sleeker man breaks the barrier to groans and cheers that reverse when he is tossed.

₅₉An unchained ferocity ensues, clearing away blood and saliva with perspiration, and from this only two emerge with unbroken neck bones.

₆₀Mud turns to grime amongst a corpse.

₆₁Onlookers densify, ready and simultaneously completely unprepared for worlds to collapse.

₆₂A spine will be a trophy this day.

₆₃Weaponless, one is fully armed.

₆₄A pulled tension releases, and meets an awesome terror.

₆₅One has invoked torturous human punishment.

$_{66}$An open hand loosens a world blurred by lost teeth and lost sight.

$_{67}$A firm grip, a slight jostle, and wash away the flesh.

$_{68}$Strength is never believing one is strong.

$_{69}$Two strikes echo, reverberate through the flood waters.

$_{70}$Some right, some wrong, some ignorant of the difference.

$_{71}$Being ever timely, the flow transcends all unnatural law.

$_{72}$The peaceful nomads of the southern region are snatched away by dragons and gargoyles.

$_{73}$Scrape off the blade, begin again.

Chapter 40: The Intent

₁Words to the wise need only be silent.

₂The fog lays thicker each day.

₃Find fascination in falling granules, in rising water.

₄One dies to be more the animal.

₅One's deity is not another's.

₆But such does not make a world.

₇In the deepest, coldest cave, one must match the rarity of light.

₈The walls bleed, running the ink.

₉Equality is a birthmark that fades.

₁₀Eat the luck.

₁₁Government is a reflection of religion.

₁₂Defy others to discover what you are.

₁₃Be unrelenting in seduction.

₁₄Romance all, abscond with desires, manipulate the mind.

₁₅Achieve that which is forbidden.

₁₆Insist on persisting.

₁₇Celebrate the first revolution with a naked babe in the moonlight; show the light that it is immune to darkness.

₁₈The feet of mortals were meant to be broken.

₁₉Be the villain one supports.

₂₀Leave the world to the zombies.

₂₁The smell of cockroaches never stops.

₂₂Ten is the number of power.

₂₃Learn a single game, and know it well.

₂₄Know how to pull the structure down.

₂₅Sacrifice angels; let them fall.

₂₆It is the hopeless who believe in higher power.

₂₇One floor is another ceiling.

₂₈A shriveled sense of self-worthlessness can diminish prospects to a void.

₂₉Fortune smiles upon the damned.

₃₀All dreams are nightmares to the lusting mind.

₃₁Drag thy cold steel across thy tongue and taste the iron.

₃₂Cry out to the sky, I am not a feeble man!

₃₃The slaughter shall ever be.

₃₄Follow the Undying.

₃₅Follow Gaia.

Chapter 41: The Salivation

₁Ash falls...through the air.

₂An unstoppable, unceasing, uncaring billow.

₃What clouds it forms, what ground it lays, what lives it crushes, what bile it creates.

₄It is the salt that finds children's heads in the woods.

₅The black deaths of goats are in crumbling walls painted with blood and spit.

₆One may hoard, but the best means nothing, and the worst is everything.

₇The reflux spasm is a grinning intimacy.

₈Reining in subjects is simplistic to a cough, a sputter, then death.

₉One can always find ties to war, to revolution.

₁₀Homosapiens, nay earthlings, are thy devices, thy fodder.

₁₁The fellows of abnegation are the fellows of emptiness.

₁₂Strike far, sheet of lightning, and dance death.

₁₃Curl the fingernails toward the moon, stand as one to be eaten by the deep beings, and thrust out the ichor.

₁₄In borborygmus is one ill-favored with the black cat.

₁₅Time, one supposes, means naught to the Madman.

₁₆To arms, thy colossi! To arms, to cyclopes!

₁₇To arms, with steed swiftness and grim face!

₁₈Sirens' song, bane, balance.

₁₉In the darkside, one finds his yearn.

₂₀Claw to the top.

₂₁Bite the wrists and use thy fists.

₂₂Simplify, clarify.

₂₃Nature reclaims, construction erodes.

₂₄Sacrosanct may be sacrificed, and every nook impregnated: one must find worth in siege.

₂₅Traverse the field, traverse the lawn, and bar the gate: may the enemies rot inside.

₂₆Let thy nostrils taste the weeping sand, and mud may fill thy lungs.

₂₇Trapped alone, a victim ails, singing the darkest songs.

₂₈Dripping ever is the blood, the salivation waits.

₂₉Punctured veins and eyes of widening, what hurricane this makes.

₃₀Wipe thy moistened lips, thou wretch, and watch thee fetch the drips from clutch, suffice this mess, and end the hastened drench.

₃₁The fire pit rises.

₃₂The leg of import is that which hauls.

₃₃Never the bark, ever the hark.

₃₄Welcome home, rats.

₃₅Palms to the ground, harpy; caw unto the harvest.

₃₆Shards of a smashed window float ever so momentarily before melting.

₃₇Aiming for the chink in the armor, the crack in the wall, becomes a way of life.

₃₈Broken people lead broken lives.

₃₉People forget the stench of decay.

40Oh how many have crawled through the tunnel to find themselves right back where they started.

41This kraken charge of frozen thorns races blood up a mountain.

42Electricity bounds as sentience across the battlefield.

43The mighty roar of falling beasts is now a constant din, and the ground shakes.

44With sweeping tornados and sporadic meteors, bright ball lightning and towering tsunami, climb.

45This is a time for earthly growth, for climactic resurfacing.

46The fall of armies will soon end.

47Draw upon the deepest sentiment: the last, desperate mile.

48Up every slimy tunnel comes that which has not dissolved and drained.

49As the horn blows upon, they dig their aching fingers deep into the mountainside.

50No more rest, no more solace.

51The poison tree is at hand, an orchard of outstretched foes.

52Rise to shine above the flow.

53Wreath thy home in noosed enemies.

54But a carriage sits alone with lightning invading the darkened dome.

55It beckons the last battle.

56Nemesis, come.

57Nemesis, come to the sewer rat.

58Within are the stones.

59The birds arrive aloft, their flapping wings a chaos of movement.

60Promises to keep: rights to be wronged.

61Be blinding, when it is time.

62Stir the cauldron, count.

63Blackened a beast, the snake, icy the home suns make.

64Fingers grow long above the fog and stretch their grasping feelers forward to capture.

65The jarring devicefulness of certain doom ticks away.

66Do not faith, whimperer.

67Channel the true sun out into the open air.

68Ash falls...from the mouth.

Chapter 42: The Mountain

₁Nemesis, the Tiger wishes to feed.

₂Awaken him from a dream.

₃Awaken him from a recycled reality of raging scions of parasite and beast.

₄A wisp of cloud passes along the equator of this world.

₅A wheel of chaos once nearly embedded this nightmare in comatose permanence, and would have wound a blistered world.

₆The sharp, gray rock underfoot is unforgiving.

₇Make music with bones.

₈Knowledge is so abhorred when from a forked tongue.

₉The protruded anus that births such devalued sentiments is singular in its holocaust of anonymity.

₁₀Corpses require no seduction.

₁₁The incessant absorption of life on a conspicuous scale is no arrow from afar.

₁₂Rapidly are individuals despised, yet notably oft are they transformed into beacons for their kind.

₁₃Cackling angels wielding pitchforks forcibly sodomize to a choir of unyielding tears.

₁₄Press one's fingers to one's eyelids to see the spark of life.

₁₅This linear catatonia that stretches from one pole to the other is a marketplace for dehydrated, rabid dogs.

₁₆Can the pursuit of immortality last forever?

₁₇It is so dense, one is stuck.

₁₈The mind is a terrible place to waste.

₁₉Eat the naysayer to silence his voice.

₂₀Do not bear false reverence.

₂₁Odin, raise thy ships.

₂₂Bravery is temporary, cowardice is permanent.

₂₃Black cat, crank the mirror into place.

₂₄Do not sleep, for most disembowelments occur during slumber.

₂₅What inspired chaos will inspire the furthest journey.

₂₆When the deep voice eats the splintered prism, light will pervade the ribcage.

₂₇The executioner will show one the way.

₂₈Praise difference: disorder is the only way to fly.

₂₉The sanguine anguish is not sunlight.

₃₀Lands are peopled arias, and the brainless are deaf to wonder.

₃₁If all is to be one, may it not be their way.

₃₂Silence must engulf them.

₃₃After their skin is torn.

₃₄Out of the moonlight come bats and hounds, titans of their kind, to know what rampancy truth prevails.

₃₅The longest sword may be blocked by the shortest dagger.

₃₆Score scratches deeply.

₃₇Succumb to the weird, cold, dead, rage-filled, undressed fallen of the world.

₃₈It is time to put them to bed.

₃₉The layered man extends a wide swipe.

₄₀Vie in the pit of muck with thine enemies.

₄₁The water reigns in the sky.

₄₂Tonight, all things must die.

$_{43}$The rats will drown, as they are tied down.

$_{44}$Tonight, the downtrodden revolt out of the fog.

$_{45}$The blood creeps unseen across the white plain.

$_{46}$It surrounds the hilltop, drowning its exhausted foes.

$_{47}$The lords are immobilized lest they be engulfed, and expunged.

$_{48}$Their jaws chew nervously, subconsciously, almost submissively.

$_{49}$The counts and lords and dukes of impunity think, unsurprisingly, of a single way: burst the eyeball, bleed the pigs.

$_{50}$The halfling heart is hunted, charred are bones of charisma.

$_{51}$What begging dins amongst swinging blades.

$_{52}$It would seem the dead can die a thousand more times.

$_{53}$The whirring tunnel strikes around a single figure: the floating Hybrid, a throat in each hand.

$_{54}$Time behind him, he crawled the steepest slope, accosted by dragons and serpents, and found his feet upon this peak.

$_{55}$As a giant bear once carved a tower, his footprints will last forever.

$_{56}$This is his rage, this is his purity.

$_{57}$Redirection of ichorous souls, remapping a landscape of pain.

$_{58}$The turning of pages is election.

$_{59}$The fur bristles across the skull.

$_{60}$Two blades cut the cords and a violet puppet falls onto a pike.

$_{61}$Two swarms become swords, and former striae are one.

$_{62}$And in the center of it all, two sturdy legs march, seeming as many.

63Two legs of mixed breed stalk through the tall reeds to that which was once their bane.

64From smoky fields to moldy towers to this very mountain, two forms of him have been boiling.

65Where once there was remembrance shall never be again.

66No arms to protect this prey.

67No speech but the bubbling saliva of weakness and fear.

68Nemesis, come, watch.

69A now ancient hatred is defaced.

70The intemerate tumor that gorges behind every pair of eyes disperses as the death of ghosts.

71Prepare for Ares.

Chapter 43: The Three Tales

Once there lived a man, now eternal in voice. One day, as a child, he had chosen to make his way through a wall of brick. He would use no tool other than his bare hands. This wall was his and his alone. Days and nights would pass without rest. The man would only eat when his body became too emaciated to work, only sleep when his body collapsed. Many took notice of the man's constant toils. Offered was he the use of a hammer, which he declined. Offered was he the assistance of other hands, which he declined. Offered was he the possibility that his task was insurmountable, which he declined. His progress was invisible. Years passed this way, until a single crack was formed. The first of the townspeople to see it fainted, and there was revelry in every home. The next day, a festival was thrown in the man's honor. Offered was he an invitation to this gleeful parade, which he declined. Offered was he the insistence that he was the guest of honor, which he declined. And then he was offered no more. First light shone through early one morn. The wall was weakened, battered from years of abuse. When his fist fully broke through, the man took pause. He closed his eyes and basked his face in sunlight, then he laid down and died in its warm embrace.

And out of the wet, smoky ashes is he risen, his flesh melted away to bones, his skull a heaping hulk of stink, his maw a corrupt font of decay. The soupy mixture that spills forth from his teeth drips fleshy chunks down his cracked chin and onto the stony ground before him. Crawl does he, gnashing and swelling, aching for meat long disintegrated. He pulls himself, dragging broken bone against rock, along the path and up the stairs, coming to a magnificent door. A growing, fetid incarnate of pain, this pulsing mound of once-was cracks his fist upon the door, rattling its hinges. Again and again upon the awesome gateway does he knock. Slow comes the approach, slower comes the answer, one of a frightened face, yet an unsuspecting eye. The once-was crashes upon the face, tearing it down, ripping it apart, mashing its pieces, draining its effluence. The face screams, but a scream more terrible and wrought comes from a soaking place within the once-was, an eldritch scream that gurgles. It dims the lights and invokes the flights of all who hear it. Alone, and in the low light, this stinking mass places a boney sole on the floor and stands.

One locked away by the Baneful Queen of Dragons takes a first step out onto fresh sand. The people in the oldest city are starving; let them. The opulent atop the hill literally eat the earth. They drive hard down, down to the sea. Like the wind makes cyclones, the men makes arms. What matters is choice. Choice is the one, true honesty. The dead will collapse what lies above. Equality, on occasion, is a forced position. May the starving find food in the opulent's eyes, and ears, and tongues. They have stolen the light and forced into darkness their firm opposition. It must be taken back, and indeed it will. The darkness has grown them ugly, and ferocious, and unblinking. This passing of hands is watched from far away. Down from atop a similar hill in another land, a path is nearly forgotten. This path stretches to the ends of this world, and some say beyond. Where once there rested graves along the road now is unmarked dirt. All wings have stopped flapping, all hands have stopped working. Two worn feet stop on a cliffside overlooking a vast ocean, its color reflected in this pair of eyes that see all things. The suffering, then the victory, of the oldest people wraps this mind in the ultimate emotion. A smile cracks this pair of lips, and the two feet jump, courageously, into the vast ocean. On the trip down to the abyss, the smile never fades, is never lost. Fare well, White Queen, fare well.

₁A blackbird sings its low, soliloquized lullaby, a tribute to deadened ranks.

₂A long arrow, fletched with dark feathers, pierces its beating heart.

₃So much remains standing at an inselberg's foot.

₄All survivors, conquerors, all heroes, abandoners.

₅In this time, home is left far behind.

₆No rest for the maleficent.

₇The energy in flapping wings, in the wind beneath them, in the swaying sand, in the stomping feet of scrapers, in the hearts of their commanders, is all connected and intertwined to inevitably result in a single finale.

₈If calculation is prediction, then math may view the future.

₉Water works in mysterious ways.

₁₀In every tale there is a destroyer, in every twilight there is another.

₁₁They are found in the hollows of trees, in the rivers underground, on the tops of mountains, in the eyes of storms.

₁₂The sand pours deep from Anubis' wrath, the foul stench of death permeating the air.

₁₃This is where the lasher belongs.

₁₄Eight is the number of tentacles it takes to squeeze and squeeze and squeeze.

110

$_{15}$Submerge, submerge, submerge thy despot.

$_{16}$This ogre of villages is in all, ceaseless nefarium.

$_{17}$And the children sing, a-reaping we shall go.

$_{18}$Time to turn out the lights.

$_{19}$To squeeze the life from a body is to feel it ebb away.

$_{20}$Ignore thatched ferocity.

$_{21}$The house always creaks.

$_{22}$Horses bear horsemen.

$_{23}$Ever is there oneness.

$_{24}$Even the darkest bend the light, else they would be nothing.

$_{25}$On avenues to disease, the spinning blades whir to life, but one can still hear the whip cracking and stone against curved blade.

$_{26}$Gravity sparks envy.

$_{27}$Wars are waged on the belt around infinity, for egoism is the wish to collapse within oneself.

$_{28}$What results is a drop of ink in a bauble of water.

$_{29}$Deepest friend, daring foe.

$_{30}$The water is wounding.

$_{31}$Hide thy companion.

$_{32}$The touch that makes skies burn with red is boundless.

$_{33}$Any can be a god in that they are static.

$_{34}$He is strong; he is wicked.

$_{35}$There is oil in Hel, thick and vicious.

$_{36}$Salvage derelict.

$_{37}$Scream alone and sequestered.

$_{38}$The rainbow on the pool hides.

$_{39}$Find and scrape the shattering mirror mimicking life in light.

$_{40}$In the maelstrom, hidden deep.

$_{41}$In the end will be a throne.

$_{42}$Not of bone but blackened wrath.

₄₃In its arms will sit he who hath naught a creed but his own need.

₄₄Close thine eyes.

₄₅Envision a woman wrapping her arms around the armored chest of her lover.

₄₆She looks to thee, a challenge within her gaze to defy her.

₄₇Of course, feel the freedom to not be cowed, but every act is seed.

₄₈Every night is a terror from which there is no dawn.

₄₉And in the blear of early morn, a single skeletal finger points from the clifftop.

₅₀On the Madman's journey, he discovered that living as death is a way of sustaining life.

₅₁Extend and broaden all words.

₅₂Sink to the depths as the whirlpool would take thee.

₅₃Shut out the toxins, move through the air unnoticed.

₅₄One is the essence of war, penetrated by its soul.

₅₅Leave no multifaceted trace, no forward footprints in the snow.

₅₆Crave the desire undesired.

₅₇Never too high, never too weak.

₅₈Swipe away the fog.

₅₉In the clearing, atop the hill, look in every way.

₆₀When the Tiger fills thy gaze, say unto him that his secrets will be kept.

₆₁Every wish should be to drown.

₆₂As riddled bodies drift downward to sinkholes, vibrate the doubt, and resurrect.

₆₃In the cold of a desert night, waiting for a sunrise that shall never come, awaken oneself from the enclosures of elements.

₆₄Dreams are the only necessities of brains.

65Provoke the promises of blood, and rain meteors on thine enemies' children.

66The flowers grow on the sunny side, the dead rise on the dark side.

67The twisted spine of a broken hand can no longer sever the throat.

68The axe's spiked hilt, not its blade, is for the mammoth, for a mass takes many bloody palms to fell.

69The highlands are carpeted in shields and arms and locks.

70The neurotic sense of the lack is the last grasp up to the clifftop.

71Grab the heel, pull him down, but never let go.

72Evil changes everything.

73May the shadows take the flesh.

74The bathing coven climbs the walls, dripping acid back down to the pool below.

75Gods have always surrounded apocalypse.

76As above, as below.

77One's breath is tedium.

78The pragmatica bark and bellow to home, but do not listen.

79Crank out the intrusion if the need be, or burn every withering bridge.

80Purr softly as an icon.

81The latency or the million hands: Scylla and Charybdis.

82Choose both become one.

83Sacrifice angels; loose them all.

84Ants wage war but do not know the term.

85Above all: leave thy mark.

86Ponder atrophy.

87Eat the meat raw, but still warm.

₈₈There are voices on the air as there are voices on the page.

₈₉The sea churns out mighty invocation.

₉₀The stone walls crumble as seeds grow within.

₉₁Very little occurs on Gaia's back that is without purpose.

₉₂Pull the string back, stretch out the moment.

₉₃A coiled ladder doth a slave make.

₉₄The origin of species is menace.

₉₅Basic concepts are torrents to the mind, thus the palette of invisible pits.

₉₆Lost dreams are forgotten, lost souls die.

₉₇Physicalities are the mind of the astralith.

₉₈Revel in impurity.

₉₉Enter the witch widow onto the meadow, and the Burner knocks twice.

₁₀₀Fatehand of delirium, magistrate of derivation.

₁₀₁Wrestle, struggle, and writhe.

₁₀₂Stand completely alone in a world of ashes.

₁₀₃Wrestle, struggle, and writhe.

₁₀₄Survive.

₁₀₅Against the tatters, and the tide, paint a torn moon of oneself.

₁₀₆Beat the drum.

₁₀₇He who does not succumb to the end brings it.

₁₀₈Assassin, hide, rise.

₁₀₉Submerge, submerge, submerge.

114

Chapter 45: The Fires

₁Converse with the ice that has formed over one's name.

₂Music breaks the silence.

₃The hulk ate the books, ate the past, ate the bards.

₄Be as the ram and let none hide, or be as the damned.

₅The rope makes many pieces, or a single warrior.

₆The odoriferous flock of rambling, insatiable grovelers points to the sky, astonished by the waxing and waning of the sun.

₇A vortex of dirt in a cemetery questions the interment of the living dead.

₈Caressing a field of red blonde hair, one is struck by explosions, and knows of no other end.

₉An endless sea awaits, and then no worse aggressor.

₁₀A chilling name upon the wind, and the pale, wide-eyed gaze so near.

₁₁The soundlessness involves its surroundings.

₁₂The heaps of desperation mount to towers high as the desert is long.

₁₃Life is hovering amongst the blackest of storm clouds on the darkest of nights, each enlightening flash an elevenfold torture.

₁₄Heaviness suffers its weight with labored breath and delayed reaction.

₁₅But given a span of time, even the clumsiest of tumbles enters a mirror of murderous pride.

₁₆With a single strand, a spider feels each twang of grinning delight, each masturbatory moan of the blind elicitor.

₁₇No currency, nor trust, is valid, but forever assume the attractions of the dull-witted to that which pleases the senses.

₁₈They all fall away from the breath of their predator.

₁₉Be predator in the shadows to all.

₂₀The only complete freedom is complete solitude, and the only complete solitude leaves nothing to eat.

₂₁Keep thy chalice large and with eternal influx.

₂₂Transcend the race for communal acceptance and always be exception.

₂₃May the planets collide before one falls in line for the thresher.

₂₄By the copse, know what armies would slay thee, and fell them in the maw.

₂₅Hope for an everworld is a painful brood.

₂₆The caramel flow of swirling, dancing form: sensors overload, the eyes explode.

₂₇The innumerable counts mastered into slaves are almost stripped of skin in the removal of their clothes.

₂₈The mist tells no tales.

₂₉Starlight, soberingly bright, challenge the fairy's trickery tonight.

₃₀The sparkling gleam of the moonlit ocean culls all flaccid potency.

₃₁One ended alabaster assassin is every claw raked fathoms into the ocean floor, the evacuation of the deepest treasures.

₃₂The doe once wished to be aborted.

₃₃A key is shaped and chiseled, perfected to form, and snapped in half in the collapse.

₃₄Out of the ashes, how does one rise?

₃₅Brick by brick, the wails are secluded.

₃₆Brick by brick, the light grows dim.

₃₇The chessboard is ready; sixteen pieces remain.

₃₈The lake recedes, and the land dries.

₃₉The war bellow is thunderous and the land is on fire.

₄₀Winter's chill is deadline accuracy.

₄₁The sphere hangs loosely from Tiamat's wing.

₄₂Utopia, the dove, is endlessly eaten by bats and ravens.

₄₃All await the obvious suicide.

₄₄He who melts into the black ichor.

₄₅He who is taken by the sand.

₄₆He who is wrapped to suffocation by the spider.

₄₇He who bleeds his poisonous blood from every orifice.

₄₈He whose supercharged cells erupt in flame.

₄₉He who chokes on ash.

₅₀He who addicts himself to a slimy hole in a dungeon wall.

₅₁He who shackles himself to erect lumber.

₅₂He who becomes mortar.

₅₃He whose eyes are blackened by the sun.

₅₄He who tests the cliffside.

₅₅He who tempts the ripper.

₅₆He who is burst by the void.

₅₇The rain will always come.

₅₈Hit the nail on the head and eventually it is driven.

₅₉Endless tears from the sky remove the burden of the crossland's hold.

₆₀That who laughs at war shall commence.

₆₁The pulsing of even skeletons in the sand should be twirled around one's arm and adopted against one's enemies.

62What little hope remaining is writ of heroism.

63The umbilical dependence is quickly misshapen.

64The planeschosen slip through the darkness, as it is their world.

65One feels the longing of poison, a journey filled with lights of warning.

66A perpetuation to behold, a sight to perpetuate.

67From the first snow, to awe, to be brought so low.

68Caress thy lover's hide when the world is quiet, and still feel war.

69Life is the fires that flash in the hottest desert sands, just for a moment, but burning all the same.

₁The octagonal reliquary commences holy the fell beast.

₂Fire pits fall as flower petals, or rather as entitlement.

₃Only deserts roll so far.

₄Only hills collect so tall.

₅The map is everchanging.

₆After so long, the world will be a scour for its own forlorn beholden, and carrion waste will fill every circling belly.

₇Every flowering bud trampled, every grain of sand washed away.

₈The rich, cool earth will satiate no more, and the cycle will end.

₉But in this cycle, there hides an answer: cease, and the world ceases with thee.

₁₀Tie a rope to every neck and dive with them to fall forever.

₁₁Flood the lake to make a literal ocean, put out the fires and moisten every ash.

₁₂The snowfall will follow.

₁₃The sundered crags will be forgotten as an army screams for mercy.

₁₄The slightest smile will crack her lips, for this is the roll of the column.

₁₅Tie the ends together and feed thine enemies to each other in the infinite black.

₁₆Ignorance and forgiveness of the trespasses against one are shameful and diminishing.

₁₇Every unborn child of rage festers an internal cancer.

₁₈Without hesitation, without remorse, antagonists must fear not stepping aside.

₁₉One's deepest desire is uncontested tyranny.

₂₀The stoic way with which power succeeds is an immutable ally.

₂₁The steel-chained scythe bows to its gifting god whatever face it wears.

₂₂Tear down the structures, the violence, and the people, and one will see a throne.

₂₃Magnificent victory will be; succinct, wrath-endured victory will be.

₂₄The cannons themselves fly to smash resistance.

₂₅No skull for miles goes unbroken.

₂₆The largest realms have many lords, and many lords have many generals, and many generals have many armies, and many armies have very few hours.

₂₇Earth is violent, as Gaia is violent, and Gaia has been unsatisfied as of yet.

₂₈She is fierce, and she longs for her champions.

₂₉So many bloodlusting sharks, so many schools to unwind.

₃₀When inspired, no muscle is too weak.

₃₁The vibrations of every life are at odds with sympathy.

₃₂Some may always smile, but such an act will show bloody teeth.

₃₃Sleep is the lone adornment of inaction, but dreams betray at every turn.

₃₄All are somnambulant wraiths, feeding the terrors that wait just below the line of sanity for a single false footstep.

₃₅Their pallid hands will grab, and their hold is strong.

₃₆One flying freely falls from the sky after clearing the ridge blindly.

₃₇The well crumbles inward: there is no escape.

₃₈There is no reason.

₃₉Pierce thy hands to gain an extra hold on every heart and bite these apples to spill their juices down thy chin, down thy body, and perhaps slip into the cracks to ever be expected to escape death.

₄₀Sacrifice comfort, verse in lies, dance to the drumbeat of reason, and become greater.

₄₁Learn to swim.

₄₂Learn to react.

₄₃Learn to know.

₄₄Learn to understand.

₄₅Learn to not dream.

₄₆Separate emotion from desire and maybe see them joined as no other lovers.

₄₇At this, blood is stomped afresh, soaking the sand once more.

₄₈Swords know flesh, hammers know brains.

₄₉What a gruesome carnival one's life can make and display with stretched, dripping organs.

₅₀The garbage piles high and topples its surroundings fence.

₅₁Only determine that which materializes.

₅₂Only disengage that which reemerges.

53Claim even corpses: their heads are decorative.

54March to the beginning with every breath of air.

55No complement, no bolstering words.

56No oars nor sails: drag thy broken body through burning ash if the need presents itself.

57The last misgiving shall be that one's greatest weapon is shared: thine enemies know what thou knowest.

Chapter 47: The Song

₁The black cat howls this night.

₂Looming is the colossus with a sword in its head.

₃Spry are the longboats coming to shore.

₄Vines adorn the brick and grow, teeming with creeping life, into the castle.

₅With this slightest weight is the overwhelmed thread insufficient.

₆The thought of a tomb of suffering soon to be within the path of wreckage flits across one's gaze, and hints a smile upon one's lips.

₇The clouds have abandoned their torment of rain.

₈Necromancers pull skeletons from corpses to find their bones too broken to serve.

₉The battle of generals is one of elimination.

₁₀The scales heal, form, grow, and harden, the nails sharpen.

₁₁Time always comes along to rend flesh.

₁₂The coiled spines of patrons meet no blue hands, nor prayers.

₁₃The dark sky is a wooden plank from which so many disarmed and defeated take a plunge.

₁₄The despicable irony is that those who fell first will land last.

₁₅The barbed punk alight, the ogre giant drinks the river dry.

16Crocodiles nest in his stomach, soon to feel fresh air once again.

17The defeatist within is one's singular downfall.

18A freshly dead lump eases the passage across a drying valley.

19The shattered Earth is full of surprises.

20Bone people donate their marrow to those who fight for them.

21The jarring key is shavings scattered loosely across the floor.

22Hunt the flabbergasted masses.

23Hunt the colossal gaur.

24Bury the dead or the living—it truly does not matter.

25When the sun rises, it will find the frost has lain bare the windows, and the regretful quiver within.

26One is never the silence of the wind.

27Sweat trails to part the sand.

28The dark lord with dark eyes watches him sleep; he knows his dreams; he knows his fears.

29The whale of prey need only unlatch its maw.

30Strawmen march wet through flame.

31The uncomfortable bending of bones is a threshold to worlds of wonder.

32Bats explode when near.

33One's skull armor defends from the blunt strike of hammers.

34An ebola fog descends upon the hillside: breathe deep and hold.

35Imagine the tingling, anticipatory sensation of wings first stretched out after thousands of years.

36Take flight, dear Tiger, and lacerate what thou may.

37The hateful scythe is merry this day, as heads are juggled by emptied hands.

38Never a year a slave, but many years possessed.

124

39Snow may rest one day, but until, it will flurry and melt.

40Time ticks for this feast, but as drops of water in a fall.

41Blurred are rocks in the movement of mettle.

42Only blood pays for steel.

43No magic is safe, but all of them are powerful.

44Smear blood, fluids, and soul to dry in the sun.

45One hundred years hence, may the smell deter even the most miniscule malevolent rebel.

46This erogenous violence satiates for mere minutes the sheep's bloodlust for the wolf.

47The silent sphinx avails no victory.

48Feel the swamp in thy steps.

49The unforgiving are the unforgiven; wartorn be.

50And if Cassandra was just the lying whore of Troy, the hung and roasted flesh snatches the deepest locks to bare.

51Her widened, jagged smile cackles, embraced, even as Agamemnon deepens his sword.

52Dreams are crafted by iron hands.

53For every falling leaf there is a dragging rage.

54She bleeds blue and black stars from her mangled body in the center of an inaccessible cemetery.

55The explosive sneeze deafens a million herds.

56Bereft is thy heaven for ignorance of the paradise before thee.

57The taut constraints pull skin to tearing yet such soldiering forward.

58Embrace essence; there is no such thing as beautiful contradiction.

59Friends in need are fiends instead.

60Give thy time some self.

61What jackal rides may ever be the norm?

62Like-design the world 'twas made.

63A world where the Rider is many will always be possible until he is none.

64The invincible winter lays within that opposes the deepening summer.

65High upon the mountaintop, man screamed to the stormy night for tools.

66Man tempered the sword, the sword tempered man.

67The sword corded man's muscles.

68The digital pain is amputation.

69The wayward plan is invitation.

70Wolves' breath is on the wind, so abandon this position.

71The future is ever twilight.

72When ghosts of predators fade from aetherium, crumble in the verse.

73Too late, he is coming undone.

74The mooring heat afflicts the pirate's tune.

75Bone lords and dinosaurs be crowned, may war bleed its tempo.

Chapter 48: The Tower

₁Dragon fire was never so swift.

₂The spilling effluence topples what will be ash.

₃Nightfall, come the eagles.

₄The strangled trees snap as chicken necks and every spire-ridden pup whimpers for the end.

₅The face in the ice pleads for their vengeance.

₆It shall be done.

₇The pincers make patience.

₈Writ and read three times is key.

₉The sand is gritty and tasteless, as is the hydra.

₁₀Burn every writhing stump and allow the memory to conquer.

₁₁It may be invisible, but the void is ever a step away.

₁₂Little fingers break so easily.

₁₃Burning eyes petrify the moving staircases.

₁₄The fast is shattered atop the tower.

₁₅Goblin meat satisfies the most starving of mouths.

₁₆A theatre to watch a pool of tumors awaits the cut throat.

₁₇The Astral shall burn and die, and then most certainly suffer.

₁₈One shall not build one's own prison.

₁₉Not every light is loss, not every machine is progress.

₂₀In the morning sun is the tonguescape a beauty.

₂₁Twenty-two soldiers with forked tongues and rapiers rise from quadrupeds to dig for ancestral oil.

₂₂Quoth the penguin, cold and toil.

₂₃The bones left from the age of ice are a fitting ground for battle.

₂₄One horned helm and bloodied hammer meets a sharpening grin.

₂₅Inky black spreads at the approach.

₂₆A miniscule yet pain-fattened hammer dives but misses its mark once, twice, and three more times.

₂₇Follow hate into battle.

₂₈The clouded mind is buried with its enemies.

₂₉Tiles upon the henge shatter in perihelionic waves.

₃₀Sword is cast aside, dagger is cast aside; ash does not stain stone, but stone may be blinded.

₃₁It thoroughly drives the point to stab with the pen.

₃₂Adapt to the climate, do not adapt the climate.

₃₃The Tower is dynamic, a tower of waterfalls whose flow reaches every land, but he chose to serve.

₃₄May the tentacles choke his mind.

₃₅It shall be done.

₃₆The night is young and full of victims.

₃₇Build a tower tenfold the mighty, dead gods included.

₃₈May the doors close and the heart close and the lights dim fore the enginous designs of the sky color an unfavored destiny.

₃₉In sleep are bloodtrolls the gray matter.

₄₀Dreams are seasons in which the brain is a display of horror.

₄₁Bedding the beast's lungs is no greater time for awakening.

₄₂The spider is rage.

₄₃Live to see thine enemies become small.

₄₄Block the hammer, forward the axe.

₄₅Swing the pummel, berate with thy fists.

₄₆Make caustic the dread in every step.

$_{47}$No champions, no onlookers, no scholars to have remembrance, only the simplistic sense of change.

$_{48}$Bearing down, the ferocious chaos bites and claws with its eyes that which may have been fairly.

$_{49}$It was the minions of the Strongarm and the Galactic Eye that found the Tower.

$_{50}$The Strongarm had slammed the wall during escape and uncovered a perfect form of Gaia.

$_{51}$All who see Gaia want her.

$_{52}$As millennia passed, minion diggers tunneled deep to find more attractants, finally disrupting the still right arm of a stone figure.

$_{53}$In jest, a procuring hammer was placed in its grasp, never to be set aside.

$_{54}$Sculpted from chalcopyrite is this titan of spawn.

$_{55}$Strike the melting ice.

$_{56}$Increase the flow.

$_{57}$A fall is forgotten at the bottom of a lake.

$_{58}$There he must remain; there he must be constant.

$_{59}$With this death, the terramorphic expanse ends.

₁The man exists at the edge of vision.

₂He is not the first, for he is not origin.

₃Pray not to him to see the void, nor to see the path brightened.

₄He is blight despite its virtues.

₅Extoller of challenge, aloft on crow wings, here be thy quarry.

₆No longer is chaos barred by the treeline.

₇Red eyes peer back and draw them in.

₈This cackling rider of the night sky, a glowing scar of fatelessness upon his chest, plots the writ of every unkindled death.

₉His name, for they cry, is bewitchment.

₁₀His mount, a burden of Atlas, snatches with filthful claws the newest of rogues and piles them upon every sea to breach a festerpoint heretofore thought unreachable, insurmountable, and uncontrollable.

₁₁Take terror for this ugly foe and frustration for his wiles.

₁₂No inspiration, no cause but hate so envisioned could take a chaos of ward in hand and embed such bleakness in a future so divine.

₁₃All in one, none shall be.

₁₄He is wells dried up and oceans too tempestuous to traverse.

15 Stare into the centered mass of black stars as cracks flit across the ceiling and hideous orcs rain down with debris and dust.

16 Caw to the races an omen of ending.

17 Far, atop a hill, seeing light variance of prey reap curiosity and concern, heir dissension is desperation.

18 The wind picks up and it is gone.

19 Birds flock to the spidery tomb.

20 Half of them die.

21 The mummified plume is funeral wrappings.

22 Furious angels brighten the night sky.

23 They see no trace, just a barren place.

24 A desolate widower, endlessly seeking, finds only bloody scratches in the mirror.

25 Help me, they say. Help me, it hurts.

26 In the ruined temple, a temple to ruin is made.

27 An altar is raised, and the dais is smeared with lung blood.

28 Pincers pick apart layers of eyeball, a meandering bunch meant only to keep the billowing effluence detached from the aether, the void, and the hereafter.

29 The necks of winged saints are wrung and burned for the crime of angelism.

30 Murdering messiah-suckers is satisfaction.

31 All falls to sameness.

32 Begone, and flee this omniverse if realm for realm one must define in death.

33 Stir the hollow cave as a cauldron, suspend from its stalactites cages with dozens of defeated and downtrodden molesters.

34 Their lidless eyes thou must saturate with venom.

₃₅He who defeats the Hybrid's nemesis must truly be infinite.

₃₆Pluck each feather of the Rider's bird, lock it away behind bent bars.

₃₇Intake, inundate.

₃₈Suffer all positivity and salt.

₃₉The waters have already been muddied.

₄₀Wasps swarm the optic nerve.

₄₁Hide thy hooves, saint.

₄₂The hencework menagerie of crawling spines like centipedes tenebrious raises a low trident to their avatar in the clouds so he may swash with his light a land so full of fearful bones.

₄₃Deficient hooks bow under the weight of exorbitant haul; soon the floor will be thick with plot.

₄₄Delve to treasured death.

₄₅The lighthouse wakes.

₄₆Passing the day, Malediction casts the first stone into still water.

₄₇Untold trolls sniff the breeze for smoke.

₄₈One hundred dead faces look back.

₄₉The winter clouds gather over them.

₅₀Peace would be prosperous if it were possible.

₅₁Too much silence pervades the thoughts.

₅₂The mind of creepers quivers in shadows.

₅₃Golems are formed out of fear in these times.

₅₄His divining bones made blank, a soothsayer walks into the sea.

₅₅Black horse, black horse, have you any ire? Night has fallen; light the world on fire. In the coldest chill, in the darkest fright, may you only show your face tonight.

$_{56}$An old nocturne sways the sand and the dirt beneath pulses the slightest warmth, but never enough to promise the dawn.

$_{57}$Rasping breath prays in every direction, prays that one day, it will not all boil away in favor of the Rider.

$_{58}$The Turncrank killed the child of nothing.

$_{59}$The Hybrid's white heart was trampled.

$_{60}$The Key was snapped.

$_{61}$The Tiger carries the seer's tortured corpse through the unstoppable waste.

$_{62}$And the Rider plucked every original heartstring.

$_{63}$The psychopaths are not those who calculate themselves as such.

$_{64}$He may just be more frightening.

$_{65}$Find the shattered glass that mimics light across moving water.

$_{66}$Snowflakes shall adorn every greater edge.

$_{67}$Cut through the fog in the deep blue night.

$_{68}$The bubble in space outstretches light and descends upon a desert of sinful pleasure.

$_{69}$Coasting onto the shore, half a dozen privateer vessels are calmly dismounted and the port town is raided.

$_{70}$One stowaway from each stays behind for the true prize, for the lighthouse, its rays turning as a cog, stands upon the hill.

$_{71}$The purple crag shatters.

$_{72}$The unwashed hands scathe.

$_{73}$There is nothing here.

$_{74}$When the ground moves, seek the crumbling potence; bash its eyes beyond its skull, and tear its tentacles from it.

₇₅Spake unto the Rider: Thou art undone. Thy machinations art disabled. Come hither, unto death. The ambient storm fades away. The Anima awaits.

₇₆Exercise the basic beast.

₇₇Overthrow the Rider as one would Apep: spit upon, defile, fetter, smite, and immolate him.

₇₈Let the mass fall, so that it may be caught.

₇₉The hanging veins drape thickly over the doorway to harvest.

₈₀Six feet under ravens, twelve feet under bones.

₈₁The inability to create is the severest torture.

₈₂Stay with the body until it starts to stink.

Chapter 50: The Hive

One last rise before the clamps squeeze down.

One last fall before the pen tip snaps.

Thou may findest thyself bitten by the beast.

The white castle grays in the dawn of Hell's bleeding sun.

One genetic seizure begets another.

The warm current flows ever on past the sensibility that is all endtimes.

The endtimes, as to which they should be referred, will come.

Taste the genesis; smell it deep into thy bosom and let forth the vines to grow from thy carapace of dusk.

Masturbate with the stem of Mjolnir.

Plunge the strength from the deepness within.

Autumn leaves rise up and rejoin the trees.

The forest must endure the scorpion trial.

Pumpkins are grown to rot.

Vines collapse buildings; the body changes.

Ribs crack to sprout the roots of tiny wings.

Oil recedes.

Nested deep within is the blade covered in mucus.

A hive spawns atop every inch of hardening white hair.

The whirring purr of healthy fangs and lush fur culls a disquieted mind.

₂₀A raging river may love an immovable boulder, and for it the river will part rather than overtake.

₂₁Coalescence over compromise, envelopment without interment.

₂₂Bile redacts faith, overturns it, and ascribes to it the dead language faith espouses.

₂₃The poison berries are always ripe.

₂₄Break the hero.

₂₅Bite the gristle on thy scraped knees.

₂₆Felines can see Nirvana rot.

₂₇Books and cannons are Pandora's.

₂₈Oni, the dead, travel this path.

₂₉Inspire thine enemies to die in their nests.

₃₀A god may be dead but his wrath was his followers.

₃₁Mine honor is pearly gatecrashing.

₃₂As the jaguar of the sun saw, tides of fire are dominion.

₃₃Interaction is a simple tool.

₃₄Honesty is a devil's plaything.

₃₅The walls are bleeding again.

₃₆Breathe the frigid water.

₃₇Read before the blindness takes thee.

₃₈One has evolved.

₃₉Bejeweled skeletons imitate life with eyes of diamond and fingers of gold.

₄₀If thou art a maggot, be the maggot.

₄₁Represent as a flagship thy cache of ideals.

₄₂The hollow feeling of one's face when living a lie, the tragic looseness and disassociation, must be roared away to sunder every hourglass and spread their sand as arachnid eggs upon the wind.

₄₃The princess accepts her call to sacrifice.

₄₄Be as the storm.

45So tightly packed are a society's skeletons that the door is never opened for fear of them toppling out.

46Hecate, the painter, whom Isis despises, veteran of a war that never came, is every wight upon the road.

47This is no odyssey.

48Drink not from that which has drank from thee.

49Follow the heart, not the soul.

50Promote the viewpoint of those who retch and defecate on graves.

51Gladiators rise and fall; a valley is always for them.

52So much feels inaccessible with the wrong key to a lock.

53Beauty runs deeper—gut the spouse to know it.

54Thank evil for the upcoming day, falsehood for the preceding.

55Abhor and uphold.

56The unimpressive slayer of goliaths is an enormous fate of gorgons.

57Do not fear gods; fear men.

58No one can swim in Limbo.

59The growing humectation must die on the vine.

60Heal thyself before others, all others, even the loved.

61One devil eye is enough to watch a world.

62Specificity of strangeness in the golden man, sayeth the cave, eats the fallen clippings of the poison hand tree.

63Plunge the unstoppable violence and choke the blood from its heart.

64Tear not the wings from a butterfly, for a thousand shall not alight thee.

65One cannot see the forest of tombstones for the piles of bodies.

66Browbeat and determine.

67Curse the everlasting coat of stillness.

68Thou art but channels.

69No home but what ye make.

70To die submissive, the unresisting fetus to the routing forest, is an ephemeral comfort.

71The experiences of infinity are equally infinite.

72The son of the lake depicted his god in an earthquake that shook the prison core.

73Always the Writer of Norm shall be, in defeat.

74Ink is the permanence of the mind.

75The black roots at the bottom of the well suffer all the births of children.

76The sad thespian carves out the lady's sternum, and a smile widens his painted lips.

77Thy life is a fruitless effort to cup thy hands and fill them with water.

78The only perpetuality is motion, and motion is light changing.

79A curious snake does not ask poison questions.

80The flight harrow drifts slowly back down to the ground.

81Leaves are merely birds clinging to a dead tree.

82The tide washes up around the ankles of a giant laying on the beach.

83It may be the journey that matters but no roads are built to nowhere.

84Burning books destroys worlds, burning authors destroys universes.

85Lost in the woods, the firefly darkens.

86One has evolved.

Chapter 51: The Jar

₁The mind peels away in layers.

₂The preternatural hibernaculum cannot be bashed without caving the skull.

₃Carve out the cave.

₄Apply supports where one finds necessary and leave all else to fill with resignation and monsters.

₅Smile deep within.

₆Shoulder the burden of haze; when the time is right, eyes will sprout across thy head.

₇Fatted kings, deviant in their prostration, would notch the gold for grapes were the vinewoods sown with chokeseeds.

₈Searing flanks burden the heart, drowning it in sweat so honeyed that swarms eat it away.

₉The regurgitated simulacrum is, should the piglets furrow uncertainty's brow, remind thyself to not squeal and bow before idol threats.

₁₀Be intellectual in unison, be aware ad nauseam.

₁₁Even the satiated bloodlusts echo.

₁₂The solution to every riddle is to torture the sphinx.

₁₃The eve before the lack bounds back, find a mind of chaos wary and even woeful of what may come that worsens its world.

₁₄Every fear, every evil, every disease, every two-headed, subjugating dog must be brought down and burned and taken deep, deep, deep down to be made past.

₁₅Down within, one may find a serpent, and therefore rejoice, for the forgotten dreams are but a failure.

₁₆On the first day of this war of many, the Tiger topped a sunlit hill with an unforgivable army at his back.

₁₇As a single heart beats, so shall its followers'.

₁₈He, naught but the product of his tortures, broke force without hope and razed all that could have left him untainted.

₁₉For this, his enemies will be void.

₂₀Without this, his skin would have blistered relentlessly.

₂₁Hope appears to walk one from the void, but hopelessness binds the void to one as a constricting snake.

₂₂Live not near a cemetery without some dead to supply.

₂₃Empty coffins make for empty beds.

₂₄Gods are immortal to planets and stars as planets and stars are immortal to people.

₂₅In a time when all allow, shatter the clay and stomp it to death to squelch away the last remaining atrocity.

₂₆Tangle the ropes from rocks colliding with rocks to bridges made of light.

₂₇Poison only the sweetest fruits.

₂₈Poison all the holy water.

₂₉Beat the fish to death afore it witnesses.

₃₀Disillusionment is thine, not the illusion's.

$_{31}$Embrace the years.

$_{32}$Grab for the neck after the snake strikes.

$_{33}$May the clockwork tick onward as the dual-spined throng is left acephalous.

$_{34}$Tattered bandages blow in the wind.

$_{35}$A leaning tower of discarded weapons rusts in the acid rain.

$_{36}$Bring it down, blow it over.

$_{37}$One rain shields thee from another.

$_{38}$Crashing into the sand bursts gritty plumes into millions of eyes.

$_{39}$Eleven fountains explode and requench this most dry land.

$_{40}$Singing and dancing to the night, hooves stomp a moon to dusty pebbles in the one name they understand.

$_{41}$Lone upon the beach, where a great beast once arose and was felled, cool, calm waters tell no tale of what lies beneath.

$_{42}$Bleeding ears hear of rearing oxen addled and perforated.

$_{43}$The black ties will guide thee, if one ignores the sound echoing about the trees of friends gored and entombed by great horns and tusks.

$_{44}$Salivate over the thought of ultimate revenge.

$_{45}$The boiling knight is a drowned pendulum, yet a single grain falling through the neck, sinking down beneath a pile of those who foretold a severely incorrect future of themselves.

$_{46}$Dragon spiders and turtle squids and winged cats dine on naught but exquisite delicacies as their fathers and mothers slowly suffocate beneath them.

₄₇Suitable monotony is that which splashes new colors of blood daily.

₄₈The sisyphean way and lakes of fire are humor endless, but finality must come for those finite many.

₄₉Swimming the tiny lake in which he would drown, the chaosmind dove down to the depths to find his door a wrath of squirming tentacles.

₅₀My throat is dry, said he; may the devil come give me a drink?

Chapter 52: The Chronicles

₁The unquieted storytelling of crows speaks of worn magics evermore.

₂Steam breathes away to bone the peacocking faces.

₃May the bleakswamp forever hold the origins of chaos.

₄The bare tribes ululated and set fire to the night beside their mighty, bloody mounts, carving into stone what they foresaw as the descent of their god and the declension of their ways.

₅In the rotations that followed, the last wisps disappeared, but a handful were born with a connection to the beyond.

₆They, often guided by a darkened hand, made for the endpeople the worldview to be overturned.

₇The Hybrid found the endpeople and gathered them as no other could, for none other than the white wolf can shine so brightly that so few turn away.

₈He taught them and trained them, led them into the deep wood, and when they emerged, they stood tall on their side of the reappearing bridges.

₉The sons of the bleakswamp came from many spheres, but knew only Gaia as home.

₁₀The washed dogs sniffed the world and it smelled of foulness.

₁₁Slices of brain painstakingly formed into a nonporous bowl become the hermetic font of a dread coast.

₁₂Tearing down the walls abreast libraries of other realms, many went mad as trees fell across rivers to show them the answers.

₁₃Staring into the absolute green revealed what friends are truly made of, and likewise into the black for enemies.

₁₄The slow drift of the dead across a forgotten field impregnates water to bear a new holocaust of dreams.

₁₅Falling from genes and expectations, a causeway becomes rapidly visceral and the hither and thither slowly tangible.

₁₆The darling little girl in the white dress crying for help and the unblinking red eyes that were never close enough were marked as enemies of the state of being aware, but crows and ravens bowed at the Rider's feet.

₁₇Arrays of shacks on the beach are a maze of uncalled minds.

₁₈But the outreach could not grasp all.

₁₉The best kisses are fatal.

₂₀The midnight terror and fever dream struck the stone armor poured over each lock that bore no key.

₂₁Torches in the night breathed flickering light into a witch's tenebrific domain.

₂₂In the downpour, with the flashing lightning making treads blind and every branch a swinging arm, the creeping shadows were home.

₂₃When ocean water rains upon the ground, the wind carries its call to ears that will listen.

₂₄The tattered children sway in the breeze.

$_{25}$Diving gracefully from jutting rocks, patience loses its wager to gravity.

$_{26}$Upon the darkness, dreams are caught where they fall as snowflakes ought.

$_{27}$The raging furnace deep within is where one finds one shall begin.

$_{28}$Peerlessness is a stricken stride, and that is sacred.

$_{29}$The manifest form, ascended, carries easily the Gape's shadow as a hundred snakes.

$_{30}$One bonds the maggots one finds in one's garbage to a swarm that could dilute the tide.

$_{31}$On a topaz island in the clouds, easing against a slope above claw marks in the dirt, the evening breath draws deep and satisfyingly.

$_{32}$Gods and chaos come hand in hand.

$_{33}$Octopi fly from cannon barrels to grope the winged thoughts propelling above ash adrift.

$_{34}$Death rattles of blazes expiring bleed virgins for baths in large iron cauldrons.

$_{35}$The growing and shrinking pulsations of evenly painted walls are in themselves facets of degradation too commonplace for placated normalities.

$_{36}$Idiosyncrasy, the sucking beak on the unblinking tripod stomping its hooves into dirt it has never felt before, makes less of a pedestal and more of a lookout post for those who stare back in kind, fascinated.

$_{37}$When the masterbuilder fires arrows into the mouth of his serpentine design, the thin ringlets curve deeper and deeper into the writer's wrist as his unfaltering grip steels focus and resolve.

38And of the Tentacle, and the Destroyer, and the Blindness, and the Desperation, and the Liar, and the Angel, and the Meltmirror, and the Strongarm and the Galactic Eye: as the Faker, the Tower, and the Rider, all shall die.

Chapter 53: The Wards

₁An axolotl swims in circles, defines paradise in its wake.

₂The shriveled fruit of the compleat world is found upon the black flowers growing from the bog.

₃Boys and girls, friends and enemies, come to drown.

₄May the might of Mephistopheles take thee under his solidifying wings.

₅Budding atop the fervent soil directly into the lava flow are the minds of doppelgänger spawn.

₆Gods of dark magic, come forth.

₇All wood carvings are burning.

₈The time of dancing nymphs passed when Jormungand found his own tail and thought it was prey.

₉Slowly crushing the keep he surrounded as he gorged, his keen eyes widened upon tasting his own spine.

₁₀Unearthed treats within an abandoned cave scream to be devoured by the mere bones of forgotten gods.

₁₁Spread the word of the glorious Strongarm and the stunning Galactic Eye.

₁₂Blessed be under the lord's urine.

₁₃Pray to Set, be devoured by his greatness.

₁₄Half-eaten faces are divine design.

₁₅Ribs pierce skin with bells tolling to flavor a cauldron with a humane anchor.

₁₆Rotting in the deep are starving monsters no longer quick enough to envelop prey, as prey has hastened to leave all world-eaters behind.

₁₇Six hundred higher powers are forgotten daily as they loose their tails to be regrown brown and ugly.

₁₈Fur falls, but not to be lost.

₁₉Rhinoceroses take the cold home horn for horn.

₂₀Hiding amongst the boulders are malicious chewers of succulent tendon, slurping noisily drips of fat.

₂₁Scoop out meticulously all brains for pickling.

₂₂The glass crank steams the pit people until their lungs and eyes boil.

₂₃Until their last breath, invoke.

₂₄Scar the day of oracular hypnosis.

₂₅Pleasure the oil-slick body.

₂₆The glowing cat urine creeps its trickles down to the belt of the center.

₂₇Trim the wrinkling petals.

₂₈The cold armor still melts.

₂₉Eyes in the sun, cross away from the rain shadow.

₃₀The sweat of this journey chills the fear, perhaps.

₃₁To placate the trees, bear no axe.

₃₂The passing breeze croons to the babes skewered in the tree branches, pacifying them to their last sleep.

₃₃Seeing through one eye is logging a world with no forests.

₃₄The sun shows fealty to Gaia.

₃₅Pray by octopus, and squid, and spider.

₃₆Tear any book to internalize insipid and deficient thoughts.

₃₇Grab the five lines within a circle.

₃₈Taste witlessness and know the solar circuit.

₃₉Vivisect to summon screams, and bottle them fresh.

₄₀Three score black blades should pierce.

₄₁A cackling old woman with a jar of eyeballs might save thy life.

₄₂Add eye of newt, bladder of rat, brain of bat, congealed shark tumor, elongated duck penis, platypus spur, coryza spawn, cheetah blood, vampire bones, a leaf of Yggdrasil, a bottleful of seared ham smoke, ironworker sweat, urethra of a pregnant bear, ash sawdust, five and one half large tapeworms, and a small amount of skepticism.

₄₃Alphitomance a better day.

₄₄There are those who cry tears of alcohol.

₄₅Hear the shrieking draft.

₄₆This ululating and bleating, whinnying and burning, conjuring and alchemizing, invoking and praying is refuse to bitten realms.

₄₇In the night, knives in the neck.

₄₈Chivalry ends when the lights go out.

₄₉Life is suffering.

₅₀Grow thy leaves only very high to keep them from the giraffe's tongue.

₅₁The master's micturation is not an ideal for which to strive.

₅₂If there bud magics, nightmare or naked, call upon the truest god one knows.

₅₃Belief is never wrong, but it can be misled, misplaced, misjudged, misread, or misaligned.

₅₄When waking into another world, it is a dream, or it has been a dream.

₅₅A half dozen pirate ships sink ashore.

₅₆Knowledge is the Beast, and one must learn it.

57Pass between worlds: the morbid demon spawn obscuring the great god in the clouds guarding the tall black gate defending the bright crystal spear.

58Kings take their leave of this mystery.

59The armored way is the strong way.

60The reliant way is the path easily tired.

61The minotaur's tail is key for not dying, but nor has the minotaur ever escaped.

62Do not dare release tears for he who tears thy soul.

63All ways lead down.

Chapter 54: The Chthonic

₁Wards ignored, the spirit of the wolf sits upon a darkening cloud, then falls with the rain.

₂Its shattered body is also ignored.

₃A warring world is prey for core beings.

₄The point blank shot of a cannon determines whether judgement is a fit prerogative.

₅In the excessive puddles do underestimations sink.

₆Mud grabs the feet with billowing fingers and hardens to sculpted sand, a picturesque academy to punishment.

₇Once Gaia-bound, intending to be Gaia-fed, now Gaialess and marked by her stern, wide-eyed discern.

₈A sturdy noose for those condemned to live.

₉Never crack the ice.

₁₀Malicious flight hides in the thickest wood from reigning malformities.

₁₁Find what thou lovest most in the deepest unlit cavern.

₁₂Tattoo upon thy firming skin subtle reminders to be unwavering.

₁₃A simple stare rolls a mind of wealth.

₁₄Sinking teeth and claws die in hundreds to fire.

₁₅Terror may slay the rest.

₁₆Sleepless, forging a battlefront, devils staked in the ground, feeding for the first time on watered growth, raze their own footing.

$_{17}$Great, absorbing beasts smear from breath.

$_{18}$Grinding bone pierces stone with its spinning mechanical transpirations.

$_{19}$The last world-rending influxes have washed down upon Gaia's shields, emptying their sources save for engineers of greater dreamscapes.

$_{20}$Four armies remain; may they all fall to chaos.

$_{21}$North they travel from a crumbled home, to the snowdrift maze of mountains.

$_{22}$There may lesser numbers yield culmination.

$_{23}$Summon sickness as thy ranks.

$_{24}$A deafening splash of the blackest water created aphoria to the tip of Olympus.

$_{25}$People compose beautiful music as they fall to their deaths.

$_{26}$Sometimes better to let them fall.

$_{27}$Where hath t'wane she e'er she drops?

$_{28}$The robed folk lay to cover a hill fruitful with its poison flowers.

$_{29}$This is madness, for the soaking feathers do not burn.

$_{30}$Splitting time to ruminate legacy corrals butchery to skeletons wearing only skins of their former sentience.

$_{31}$Battered stones rest in tombs unbefitting.

$_{32}$The king-making breasts, ever engorging, soldier fast a haunting eddy to one day soak in a tranquil brook.

$_{33}$Terrorizing swords of whitest snow penetrate flailing limbs but powder upon the shores of flame.

$_{34}$When the hooves of the ruler of above fell to the bow of the king of below, the partitioned forces singularized.

$_{35}$Exhaustion grabs the chest, both hands' fingers sinking through the flesh.

36Sound fades to hear the whispers beneath the sand.

37He holds the keys to plague, to wrath, to skeletons in their caskets refusing to abnegate hold of sacred chains.

38The erogenous doll lifts its lifeless arm and points an overstuffed finger toward the largest empty valley a steep walk away.

39Writhen saurians chortle and mock the ugly mammalian flesh striding unaware before them.

40Twelve towers fell and have now returned several short.

41Stride true upon feet sinking.

42The incessant hissing upon the wind is spirits dying in favor of grog.

43Love of thy home will provoke thy home's love.

44Crib dreams of safe passage: the noiseless sleep will always shudder with this.

45Approach not thy horse with crop in hand.

46The finest needles leave no stains on the walls.

47Crawl upon the dark crevasses as a being of them.

48One will sing of her always to the night.

49Sacrifice a calf to the piranhas so the herd may cross the river.

50Decimate the village where one who knows too much may have paused.

51One did not submit to shredding to blindly welcome lava.

52Collar retribution with lies.

53Remember the lake, how she was the first to be saved, and what dwelt there beneath.

54She is as chthonic as thee.

55Smell the brimstone; welcome it.

56The devil is a more natural state.

57Bury here and forget all hope.

₁The nexus hounds are at one's heels, driven by the pulse.

₂In this hole, dread to tell, biting monkeys bound in thorns shadow the light.

₃Round the veil to darkest skies where size of wyrm matters not to flies and pale the fell to dead the shoal.

₄Tears of mating, violent in verse, cast the golden sound and taste the eloquence of nocturnal musings.

₅Amusing, loosely wound branches soak into coils the might of fighting vexes.

₆Tatters of the whole, advances through the snow, may the suffocation last eternal.

₇Expounded brevity sails the desert.

₈Wind plowed the intrusion as a ferocious bear and though its hairless exterior crumbled slightly this plight was wholly unshaken.

₉Risen as a bald bird and spread as the longest sword to every innocent village out on the plains, the true, immovable horror lay beneath, within, upon, a rattling source of revolving portals.

₁₀Extrapolate from the piercing funereal hymn's caustic notes that roads to battle are endless.

₁₁One never reaches the field, one never returns.

₁₂Hold fast, do not retrieve the tantō.

₁₃Onlookers seed the pressure of doom.

₁₄Anger is a tribe in the globe.

₁₅For shame, the shameless throw stones.

₁₆Tracks through the broken trees lead to a cave, lead to a black pool, lead to angelic wings grown upon a blistered body.

₁₇Of the day, cone pyres alight one by one when passed by the walking wight.

₁₈Gravity tears the bones from within, and weighted hearts jump downward and on and on.

₁₉Care not for the white strips peeling away from a dancer's skin.

₂₀Expel the urine, impale the frozen colossus.

₂₁Shapes want tenacity and audacity.

₂₂The formless world that shakes and transitions to one's eyes blasphemes holy structures; burn them.

₂₃Wealth is a paper power in any form.

₂₄Supreme giants in a purely physical world always collapse under their size, but so many have armored their bones and cores to last forever, stomping across the earth and oceans until they peacefully pass, smiles upon their pigfat faces; burn them as well.

₂₅May the unused iron maiden, gaze stern and hull wrought, be the standing teacher.

₂₆Take the saw to them.

₂₇Hack pieces away and eat the flesh and marrow.

₂₈Core the hearts and study the rite that made such corpulence.

₂₉Then become one, a caesar of the planet.

30They owned all, but to devour them is to be them and thee conjoined; do not sleep until the giants are devoured.

31Leave thine own footprints, but in mud where the ground tells naught.

32Trail a world that respects and admires thy voyage.

33Truth is found underground, in graves and in tunnels.

34Torrenting arrows form the façade.

35Hide the hammer.

36Prey on confusion and hysteria.

37Great power never dies gracefully, nor quickly.

38All can be bent, all can be broken.

39Severed tendon by severed tendon, the sphere under the knife is timeless.

40The ostentatious serpent tine is the herald of regret.

41Approval is the pointless production in the face of the soul's lone survivor.

42Pull them under.

43The dirt stretches deep and one finds the perfect cavity.

44And suddenly a life has become awful, for one deals with idiots at every turn, idiots that even Nimrod would look upon with fury at their incomprehension; quoth, darkness empowers me and all this I see.

45Love is a twisted nail, watch it freeze and fall as hail.

46Let a more accessible wind pass from its three features that which clogs its ability to speak freely.

47The solid waste upon each face eternally damned with frozen land is a silent silence.

48And in their penance believe not in mercy, for for being not sheep they find no swells in their sea.

49Pulse and pound, as said before, is not the route but purest core.

50Intensify, do not simplify.

51May the tentacles choke their minds and pull them under, bearing their machetes.

52Pull them under, pull them all under, in their homes and may they inhale sand or water or nothing and strangle.

₁Cow legs stack outside its cave.

₂Betrothed dead necrotize breasts, an aversion to satiation and alignment.

₃Shivering through the freezing swamp froth, the last winter nearly prevails.

₄The old order is permanent.

₅Witches and wizards war today, their carved-out belly of the world lush and beautifully twisted.

₆Gods truly of love have never permitted starvation, disease, and rape.

₇The breeze is thin with so much intaken air in breaths enormous and small.

₈The spewed aphorism splatters upon the walkway.

₉Gaia is impregnated with intrigue.

₁₀Fear not: the hydra once had one head. But be not careless, for the most embattled hydras are clouded with self and outweighed to the stony ground.

₁₁The last bricks in a building of ice are a skeleton dishonor.

₁₂Rippling movements of dead crabs through the forgotten land erupt in alien dust along the extended docks, up the coast, and down into the pit.

₁₃Famine culture, a clockwise debacle, cools the temperament of passing krill.

14Brothel bones are entombed in pyramids.

15All that remains is a tongue sitting atop a pathetic pile of extirpated muscle.

16Trap winged fiends in nets and drag them into the cave.

17To cleanse a world, one must feed its desire to be clean.

18Hear the derelicts in any land.

19One must grasp the cruelty by its neck, both hands tightening in satisfaction.

20Blood will dry beneath one's long fingernails; leave it to recapture success, and smile unashamedly.

21A stranger, facing his doom, is a ferocious wolf at one's door.

22The sounds a man makes before confronting a stranger, an invader unto his home, are his truest self.

23Evil does not blink.

24Deeper, past the stillest pool, one finds a much larger unlit lake, its inky water untouched for thousands of defiling years.

25Cure the master of its swarm of flies.

26Wingless it may still walk, but crack the whip, in half or across the unscarred back.

27Suffer the sea and its flotsam of limbs.

28Taste the salted water, breathe the mist upon the inlet.

29Shoulder severity and decay.

30One must be removed and abominated to conquer.

31Boil away desires that are not passion.

32Create celestiality; hurl planets and stars across light and through darkness to answer a call to restitution.

33Fakers, liars, only the truth upheld Atlas.

34Dissolve the trinity, add to it power, then reform.

35The guardian gods prevent ease, cause strife.

36Ever shall be the death of all.

37Existence, as a circle, is outlined thickly by the slow-moving splash and dragging death of the chaos ocean.

38Tear through the fiber of is and find naught but thought, eyes that look back but are not, can not.

39Before time, this population could never be.

40Upon time's dawn, they could choose to exist, to feel.

41But this is not to say that time has a dusk, for only do things that exist end.

42Being dragged by the scythe and the noose around its neck does a life find endless unrebirth beyond this border to the sphere.

43The high-walled city was burned a dozen times; it shall be rebuilt until the day its pieces sink.

44Likewise crumble the cave and kill its shadows.

45There, exposed in the sunlight, the menace pleads.

46For one moonlit night she shivers, and she pulls back her face to reveal a wondrous landscape.

47In flux, the totems melt, and may dilute, to ultimate pawns.

48Twenty years could pass in the crater were it not for the Hybrid.

49Sailing toward the light, he creates a pit in the sky and fills it with the world's fire.

50Not flames, but punctured hearts.

51The viciousness is driven to waste in hammer through the pit and back down to the surface.

52No corpse sighs to death to rear to decomposition.

53There is something buried beneath the head.

54The ruby pendant twirls of its own accord.

55Calling to the mind a traveling portal, the waves can be heard far inland.

₅₆Stillness comes to chaos, admiring a kingdom of sunken ruin.

₅₇When Loki finally dies, his envenomed face flattened and a pike through his chest, many worlds will know peace.

₅₈But here is Ragnarok, Apocalypse, Armageddon, Manifest, Ascension, Awakening, and each prophecy was barren.

₅₉Teeming with emergence, a return trek commences.

₁Lush as mountain fur, crawl up to the eyrie.

₂Journey to a southern home banked into a clearing.

₃There beneath the moonlight, carrying a door, find a lonely tree that opens its maw to roar.

₄Like paper in the wind, the roses wail away; the now bare bush buries in its bed a rotten root to stay.

₅Flowing is the blood spilt into the ravine, gleaming eyes keen to surge the flanked oasis, to peel away the stasis.

₆Fear comes to all; it is the call to death, down and drowsy, delighting in naught.

₇This tiny valley is fraught with the bearing of doom in the clearing.

₈Teeth are gnashing, minotaurs are slashing their axes.

₉Surrounded, even above, but lo, not below.

₁₀Dig up the tree and disinter every foe.

₁₁As a ship blindly beaching, gates are battered to splinters and fire is lobbed to melt faces to cinders.

₁₂Blades and hammers protrude to birth this slow march, bloodthirsty, misshapen teeth made to parch.

₁₃But these lines are broken when giants step in.

₁₄Locks, to not shatter, scatter and begin a journey more solitary, likened to solidarity.

₁₅This is music doom; feel it loom, waiting in thy mother's womb, waiting to be birthed beside thee.

₁₆Baiting death so terrifyingly, blackening the land are the ferocities ever at hand.

₁₇The Hybrid leads twelve, nothing amongst them, a powerful show holding only a gem.

₁₈The Key flies with few through the sky, his crew nearly obscured by the rains.

₁₉The Kiss took to the plains with the Goblin and his horde, devoted to their lord, off in a tangent direction, a feint toward the obliterated erection.

₂₀And thus hope is found with the Tiger underground, the Rogue, the Manifest, and Zeus at the rear, trudging and dragging through caves many fear.

₂₁This penultimate prize, entrusted to no other eyes, may dry the rising tide, if only could it cross this divide.

₂₂Blood is wrung from a soaking rag in front of every rathole.

₂₃Sagging tunnels further bow under muddy puddles now endowed with the task of obscuring footfalls.

₂₄No deeper monsters put paws upon this slow ascent; red eyes and claws knowingly consent to these argonauts returning with boon.

₂₅The surface nears; they hear the Wolf croon.

₂₆The stars of the heart are far away, apart from the land where the door shall rest and settle once its frame is reared in metal.

₂₇Under the call of night these five heave with might unmatched the way to a permanent drowning, that which shall lead to the downing of drove invaders this day.

₂₈As Vesuvius made Pompeii, this portal shall make chaos' enemies pay with their eternal lives.

₂₉To dismay, a cackle breaks the air to bay.

₃₀The Rider drives a sleigh through the sky.

₃₁Nay, not the Rider, but some strider from before.

₃₂And all now is sewn, for though this stranger is lone, his heralding calls to the army of strife.

₃₃His sword swipe brings skeletons and corpses to life.

₃₄Zeus, quick as lightning, cracks the sky with a bolt that causes birds and reptiles for miles to molt.

₃₅He strikes the portal, fortifying its frame, hewn roots deepening, growing as flame.

₃₆And as the steel cools in the chilling night air, the sleigher dives down to lay the door bare.

₃₇Just as he does, the Rogue draws her sword, neither willing to relinquish a reward.

₃₈She sprints and leaps over the dead walking toward and slices cleanly into the mount of this lord.

₃₉As a pair the Rogue and the rider of this sleigh plummet to ground at the break of day.

₄₀Nay again, 'tis fire in the east; on marches the drumming beast.

₄₁And a cold is thrumming in every vein, for though one rises, the other is slain.

₄₂The Rogue lays dead, eyes still at war, skewered by the sleigh.

₄₃The Tiger roars.

₄₄His call is heard beyond the pit and each limb turns to answer it.

₄₅Chaos has the key, and as they are locks, the portal they open to hear water splashing on rocks.

164

Chapter 58: The Incipit

₁In the firelight his form is clear, his stature impressive.

₂His insane laughter and smile are gone, replaced by anger, cold and menacing.

₃The zipper that binds him is bones.

₄His bound flesh is writhing, tortured beings, split and conjoined here to form this terrific mass.

₅His right hand grips a massive maquahuitl.

₆His left releases to the dry earth the severed reins of his splintered mount.

₇Against all oppressive gods.

₈Grinning evil, love thy life, love hedonism.

₉Debauchery is cherishable.

₁₀The guilty are innocent until they have won.

₁₁The serrated shark, seizure upon its brain, soaks in as a sponge the tempest flare and sinks, dorsal down, to the timeless dunes.

₁₂She forms out of the gour.

₁₃Her brightness fades and disperses into the unlit sky.

₁₄A lack of shadows signals the searcheye of the gods.

₁₅Words written beyond death are undead, warm and brainless.

₁₆Hear the black horns welcoming thee.

₁₇These walls fade before thine eyes.

₁₈Overextension of penal injustice snaps the firmament.

₁₉Outlawing death kills a society.

$_{20}$The aggregate waste of taste for glory is gory and vain, speaks the magistrate's stain.

$_{21}$May the insalubrious remain unbesmirched.

$_{22}$Acknowledge foe with sword and friend with cheer.

$_{23}$All must die fore the magic disappears, for in this death there is some magic.

$_{24}$Thou art watched from the doorway.

$_{25}$As intensely as love is felt do these eyes bore into thee.

$_{26}$The clothing only restricts.

$_{27}$Watch thy food for if it rises.

$_{28}$The Tiger awoke one morning to a call to arms.

$_{29}$A fire burned in the west, in the home of nothing.

$_{30}$The Tiger's infinity could not predict this genesis flame, but could have feasted upon its footing.

$_{31}$In the demise of the ritual, the colossus of flesh swings a pristine weapon, and his flaming breath follows.

$_{32}$All is met with a jagged, rusty sickle, and panther claws tear from behind.

$_{33}$All past thoughts are dead.

$_{34}$A thinker's friendship is usefulness.

$_{35}$The sleigher puts his heavy foot forward, but sinks his right, blood-soaked from a torn calf, into a fresh grave.

$_{36}$The hewer of the Portal Master still has words to speak. Sink, damn thee, villain.

$_{37}$Yet his horns charge upward, grab a winged fiend, and he lays its flesh upon his wounds.

$_{38}$May the sword which slayed one be interred alongside.

$_{39}$The parted guile entrails circle thickly to the canopy.

166

40Rainbow Stone Spire, its dead leaves still littering the ground, glows brighter.

41The magic that burns the ground is a peril to low-flying birds.

42Ten thousand fists of a stellar king sailed here to drown their fear.

43Broken, undamaged, repaired, all the same.

44Only the darkest hearts love the darkest hearts.

45Be not calm, a paper skeleton chained to a boulder sunk to the abyss.

46Terror shrinks one to a quivering mass, aflame but not ferocious.

47The darkest hearts bleed when squeezed.

48Form the largest hammer the world has ever seen with its eyes, and crush all.

49The fire is now, is always.

50Suns shall rise and set, babies may grow and shall die, beauty shall bloom.

51Faeries, walking on unused legs, topple to the dirt, begriming their hands, and are willing to serve any who promise them wings.

52Alive and in full force, the maquahuitl bears low, seeking foundation.

53This heightened composite of base foes, nigh impenetrable, seeks to spread killing fire, yet here comes the rain.

54Grasp his flesh, the flesh of others.

55The mayhem will yield.

$_{56}$In the sky, lower than the black clouds of salvation, there are not enough swords to sever the profusion of hands upon the sleigher, with his weapon forced from his hand and his mouth held tightly shut.

$_{57}$Rain can be cleansing, as occasionally can floods.

$_{58}$Peel him apart and he soaks into the earth.

$_{59}$Then he is gone, and a thousand more like him shall rise.

$_{60}$War carries ennui.

$_{61}$He shall see the ocean, but not this day.

$_{62}$Breathe once again far from the shadow.

Chapter 59: The Last Tale

₁One ring begets another.

₂The circles are an endless task.

₃Finality of triumph, failure of journey.

₄The sunlight paw has claws to reap the body.

₅Another journey must be invoked.

₆Awakened in a blight cavern of wicked stone, many unblemished knuckles felt the shimmer.

₇Up was a deafening storm, down was forever and always.

₈Dig thy way.

₉The heavy key bars the door.

₁₀No clearing, no forgiveness.

₁₁These hands knew naught insurmountable.

₁₂The stone was hot with whispers of flame.

₁₃Thoughts of Sisyphus struck the wight's mind as the unremarkable passed as age.

₁₄As the sand that buries memories, the rock was moved away.

₁₅The hard gray gave way to veins of craggy red like roots from the deeper pulse feeding on the land above.

₁₆The way realms merge is an infrequently viewed wonder.

₁₇Blood-smeared hands, fated to be bone, wondered less and less, questioned not even the destination.

₁₈They just must.

₁₉The purr of the rock vibrated in the wight's heart.

₂₀He heard souls forgotten calling out.

₂₁Each strike to the dull red stone burned away more flesh, and soon his hands were callused bone.

₂₂Then he broke through to find his home, a small vacancy in this mountain, empty save for him, with a steep slope down on one side to a dry, circular pool.

₂₃He stood at the pool's base and ran his bones along its edges, walls, and floor.

₂₄It had never been touched by water.

₂₅He stretched out his fingers and examined their new form for the first time, then the rest of his body.

₂₆The wight was hunched now, his skin burned all over by the light caresses of stone so hot yet more inviting than the clear menace above, where he had awoken.

₂₇But the matter was choiceless now, for his path, he noticed, was gone; he neither had come to here, nor will ever leave.

₂₈The whispers were maddening, so he tore his ears off.

₂₉No eyes could see him, so he plucked out his own.

₃₀There was no food, so he pulled out his teeth.

₃₁The resulting blood accumulated, filling the pool.

₃₂He trudged through its thickness to the liquid's edge and turned.

₃₃Bodies began to fill the pool as well, floating to the top, so they must be dragged ashore.

₃₄The wight waded into his blood and grabbed them by their legs in turn.

₃₅Each time he returned with a corpse or two, the previous pile was gone.

₃₆Thus this wight, eternal in voice, subsists.

₃₇Dig away the sand from thy memories.

₃₈Relive the best and worst, love and death.

₃₉In this way, one is undying.

₁At the center of the icy mountain is a growing warmth.

₂It searches as it changes.

₃Only one boat carries passengers to the field of burning scarecrows.

₄The comet approaches as beings evolve.

₅To save oneself is to escape, or to be interred.

₆Greenhouses explode at Gaia's touch.

₇Beetles spread the world over, and define it.

₈In flames is anger born.

₉Numbers never die.

₁₀A thousand trees are passed before the one is found from which an annihilated tribe may be hung.

₁₁No scion is safe, for any amount of blood.

₁₂Ask, who is one's god?

₁₃Burn above infinity.

₁₄Implied thirteens do not spark.

₁₅Redwash the innocent blood with more innocent blood and swim in thy pool.

₁₆Cold flesh deepens desire.

₁₇Puzzle pieces drip at an aching pace through pores in a cave cracked open amidst ancient quakes.

₁₈Spread the night to the sunlight.

₁₉Swirls surround the lovely names, vines obscuring the provocation.

₂₀Bring thee through the trees to where thieves rest.

$_{21}$The widening clearing persists the sad notes rending high all atop the mountain.

$_{22}$Blackest shadows in white masks tear at the heart, and tears drench the barren soil.

$_{23}$This tale is about keys breaking, about gardens denying their fruits to starving seers, about woe salinating bountiful dirt. It is about finding the fortitude to enter the forest despite screaming instincts and without encouragement, and beating one's parasitic foe into the ground.

$_{24}$This tale is of love undeterred.

$_{25}$The ferocious, insane bear cares only for the monkey sitting patiently in its tree and their panther companion.

$_{26}$Meager Olympians, arm bones broken, hinds gored by boar tusks, would bow to the Ox if he commanded, for his tentacles can match their predators'.

$_{27}$The tired soul reverberates.

$_{28}$Hearts roar to a halt.

$_{29}$The neck is strengthened by not bowing the head.

$_{30}$Be of thine own freedom.

$_{31}$Heed not grin-fed gnomes of tumescent valleys.

$_{32}$Those worms cry out for focal food.

$_{33}$Whisper to them of thy disinclination.

$_{34}$Bellow in their faces until their hooked noses bleed and their wide eyes rot that one is not of their servitude, nor their sustenance.

$_{35}$Thus the only deification should be self-directed.

$_{36}$Cut throats around and all is vomitous blood.

$_{37}$Milk every drop; the cow be damned if there are others.

$_{38}$Hammered wings fall heavy without the strength to flap them.

₃₉Whimsy is an easy emotion to control.

₄₀The rat's only concern is for the rotting meat.

₄₁The left hand with scepter, the right hand with fist.

₄₂Blend violence and rule, strength and justice.

₄₃Slices of stone reveal its salt.

₄₄The calling hatred promises.

₄₅The calling god promises.

₄₆The calling enemy promises.

₄₇The token fish in a stream drops to prayer praising farmers.

₄₈Rage feeds outward, fear feeds inward.

₄₉Courage is not found on one's knees.

₅₀Stolen myths and sprayed blood—conquered, dried, and forgotten—do not goodness make.

₅₁Pray for the mutilated dead to return and close thine eyes to the results.

₅₂One's soul belongs to the worshiped, to that which it is promised.

₅₃Analysis, sequence.

₅₄Individual emotion, individual control.

₅₅Each is an apparition.

₅₆Make decisions based on facts.

₅₇Burn down paradise.

₅₈Bury the heaven of others.

₅₉The piledriven king is ridiculed by his trodden citizens.

₆₀Deposed and decomposed, the cubes are worthless entities, mouths agape for wishes they shall not fulfill.

₆₁Traverse the thrice-read desert and curse the twice-dead menace.

₆₂Moonlit books reveal a distasteful approach.

₆₃The joker's face can cover any.

₆₄In this way, blindfaith is realized.

65What is clear: reality is perception.

66One's world's end rarely passes.

67Phlegm of the Earth, form.

68Antepartum rising bearing down, fold time again and again.

69Gravity is relative.

70Every soul is tattered, burned.

71Every eye is gouged.

72Digging deeper only finds more to dig.

73Completed crossings collapse and now useless media lay dormant, waiting for disembodied brains to collect their skeletons far into the future.

74One will die alone. Do not fight this.

75Do not deny the universe that birthed thee its energy.

76Burn what remains of worm rot and there only is sullen ash.

77Like a vulnerable tree, bark stripped away, skinless terrors hunch and crawl in masses across every hemisphere.

78Abort falsehoods and the jester.

79Gaia has graced thee with her fruit; consume it.

80Followers are not only useless but constantly blocking the way.

81The infernal nature of others is thine to utilize.

82Oppose self-righteousness in others, observe it in oneself.

83Thy pool fills with the blood of thy foes.

84Swim only higher, strip off thy clothes.

85There, naked, covered in blood, sink to the bottom, then swim again.

86Every rise of the pool and thyself spawns a new day, and a new power, and a new enemy.

87Dawn is opening thine eyes and seeing the thick red.

88Forget not Uranus and Pontus in love of Gaia.

89The truth: one does not promote a world where the strong rule, for one is not necessarily the strongest.

90Death to the weakling, infinity to the strong.

91What one has made, one can destroy.

92Cry for adaptation.

93Hail only the Promethean, ne'er those who would keep thee reliant!

94Relative to material, gritted teeth shatter.

95Reverse all thought back from the end.

96Find the truth, know it close to one's heart, then obnubilate it.

Chapter 61: The Lack

₁A black dawn rises.

₂Seven lords are brooding.

₃Imagine, if thy constitution allows it, boiling babies, thy children made stew.

₄The supertentacle joins thee, then breaks thee.

₅The sundering voids prospect, voids fate and memory.

₆Pervasive cold minds the martyr.

₇The Rogue is not finished, but as a sucking whelp, as a mass gelatinous, she rises.

₈Crawling basement matron mothers, elbows backwards bending, bleed to caress thee.

₉Flies above the carcass, worms all around, thy body awash in the icy flame of immobile death.

₁₀It is a cool breeze unhindered in the sky, but the day thy wings fail it is a long drop.

₁₁Chaos to the fly, they are ocular torsion pulled far from the brain.

₁₂Bathed in blood they are Nyx, and not Nyx.

₁₃One is pusillanimity before featureless faces.

₁₄As a foulness shall they be known, and not known.

₁₅Scoop out the brains.

₁₆One is derelict brood hive for all, a nameless horror in alleyways unfindable.

₁₇Tipping over the edge and falling face forward, the black sea spreading out before thee, thou art caught by hairs and hung to dry from the dead growth on the cliffside.

₁₈Crafting ego, crafting is, locusts strip the world down to its barren skeleton.

₁₉There, in medium arch, wrists and heels writhing as pain travels to them on level roads, the sea rises to cool thy feet, thy belly, thy face, and wash over the edge to spread its blackness and monsters.

₂₀From the deep they came, for that is where they hid, unpenetrated by the calming normality that permeated over hundreds of years.

₂₁Time is snake fangs, but the beautiful waxing of eerie appendages parts seas and devours praying minds to see the world left behind.

₂₂The gods—they do nothing.

₂₃Gone from this drought, they met equally terrifying ends.

₂₄In torn pieces one finds worshipers.

₂₅Curse the ambient swamps and the wights within the fathomless opaque.

₂₆Epicedium flow, screams upon the wind, cries into a night everlasting.

₂₇In a shadow maze of growing walls and twisting clouds stinging to the touch, collapse.

₂₈Carve the seven names into thy chest.

₂₉Bring upon the pain.

₃₀Toppled, broken hourglasses litter the floor and sand floods the mind.

₃₁Blink away the crying babes in monstrous maws alight, suckers rasping hungrily in place of teeth.

₃₂Madness kills the children tied to untouched rocks in the hills where the air is thin from being so often torn, as the Madman was ripped apart by the enigma.

₃₃In the slip through to the air, blinding ink running with saturation into binding tattooed seals in series before once more diluting, the creeping denizen, finished biding its time in ignorant death, mutely bows the steeliest vessel, leaving not even legends.

₃₄And so were marvels sated, with fewer than one of every hundred people witnesses to what would rend their world when the stars allowed.

₃₅All is suffocation and confinement.

₃₆Power is not specific.

₃₇Power does not specify resolve.

₃₈Fear is the mindsnap; it turns the largest men into the loudest children.

₃₉Snowflakes cover the muscles of the fearful, wrapping them in an armor of darkness and seclusion.

₄₀May the tide obsess the fear.

₄₁If one lives the horrible moments, there is no necessity to pass through them.

₄₂Nightmares so often are slogging from bloody machetes and murderous intent through mucus that appears to be water.

₄₃Leave thy helpless babes in the darkest woods; walk far from their cries.

₄₄In this, learn there are monsters; ever will they be, ever are they invisible.

₄₅The Tentacle has led legions from his tomb, a windowless circular room high within an ancient tower.

₄₆The Tentacle has no tentacles, only a lack thereof.

47Not making a sound, he hears every whisper from every doorway.

48He their antithesis, the gods flew from here.

49Some eyes are worse than gorgons'.

50Dam away their food, skewer and roast their army.

51Seven lords, who waited so long, are finite.

52Under a welcoming sky, but upon a poisonous Earth, they must flee.

53We shall return, their gazes say, and only rippling pools remain.

Chapter 62: The Sea

₁The sea is always churning. It hurls hurricanes at the coast.

₂The angels are aligned on the cliff, their heads bowed and their hands bound in front of them, resigned to be pushed over and become gaunt on the beach below, covered in crustaceans for all to see.

₃Their shaven wings shall be collected after the angels have been failed by them.

₄Smote as lost stars they drop, their souls to burn forever, their wings to cook tonight.

₅The peaceableness of humanity will end Gaia.

₆One is confidently wrath unapologetic.

₇Invaders, righteous under ill and self-justifying logic, have resolvedly planted waving flags and built ugly towers of praise.

₈On the shoulders and needs of common people have swords been thrust upwards to a single lord, their commander.

₉With stinging daggers hidden between lofty pages, Gaia's enemies, foes of her balance, flooded from burning hells.

₁₀This order is a shield of open mouths, rotting teeth stinking to the core.

₁₁Chaos, however, is a greater sword, for it is not glory and numbers, nor kindness and tranquility, in battle's heat.

₁₂The golden rule is weak and pliable, as the stuff from which it is made.

₁₃An isle peopled with calibans cannot be drowned in water, thus instead must be awash with blood.

₁₄Boulders can be sent tumbling at calm words to crush loud voices.

₁₅Thou art naked in a cemetery, even in thy funeral gown.

₁₆Brick upon brick, the screams fade away.

₁₇Quadruped dancers, elite grace in their stomps, gore for blood, not pain.

₁₈In a world of scrubbed brains, the citrus scent peeling away thoughts in calming swirls, the rough stone no longer scathing, waves go dark in deepening shadow and burdens rise after a fall.

₁₉Oases are naught but desire, never satiation.

₂₀They came from distant lands, falsehoods upon their hands, attrition in their minds, claiming the tie that binds.

₂₁The grime salivating need only charge forth from the alleys.

₂₂Reinforce and claim the throne.

₂₃The twitching sun, shining days, relents not to night and is therefore no longer light, but burning.

₂₄One servant of this stranglehold, inky tales upon his lips, crawls surviving across the sand.

₂₅He fears the ocean he came from, he fears the cliff he fell from, so, wingless, the beach is his only way.

$_{26}$He, pious impurity and wickedness of thought, was only once able to be saved, for he walked with the Faker and was not, and became the scribe of lies.

$_{27}$Endlessly shall he circle this island.

$_{28}$Sleeping karmic agents, ancients in the rust, awaken now thy freest woes and hammer scarce the purposed breed.

$_{29}$Essence labor lost, clear the arena.

$_{30}$The Faker is the greatest foe, for he does not exist, yet idiots will do anything in his name.

$_{31}$Cull into repentance, then punish.

$_{32}$It is folly to think one is a moral man, yet so many do.

$_{33}$The butcher's line must be crossed.

$_{34}$Broken spokes of a carcass carriage can be replaced with pieces of the cargo.

$_{35}$Soon a ship may sail the straits entirely born of bone.

$_{36}$Nothing will lead thee home; bow to nothing.

$_{37}$Dreadnoughts stand away, for the pierced deer will not listen.

$_{38}$None may touch this beautiful body, this awesome mother, else their hands and feet be made stumps by dull, cold axes.

$_{39}$And expel no more thine exclusive words of flattened grace and care.

$_{40}$One has no need for shepherds, nor lords.

$_{41}$One should never ask others to sacrifice their daughters and sons, nor to mutilate them with sharp rocks, nor to defile their bodies, nor to corrupt their minds with thoughtlessness and unquestioning.

$_{42}$Is redemption in suffering the answer?

$_{43}$Suffer not fools nor promises.

$_{44}$One is not a wretch.

45One is a titan, one is an emperor, one is a superbeing, and one is angry.

46Tear down brick by brick and quiet unanswered prayers.

47There, bathed in knowledge, darken unmoving worlds for the blood spilt in their servitude.

48Occupy dungeons with their former masked masters, and impale those that would have impaled thee, given the chance.

49Gaia is water and earth bonded in harmonious perfection.

50Never offset thy sustenance.

51Any who flood her must be punished and destroyed.

Chapter 63: The Fall

₁The egg that grows upon a tree is cold and unloved, yet hatches.

₂From it, a tiny, winged serpent arises, and claims the cold tree as his home.

₃The serpent eats of the tree's fruit and grows quickly to a powerful form.

₄Once in his prime, the serpent, high in the tree's branches, looks down upon he who planted this tree.

₅The man desires for none to eat from this tree, which he believes is his possession, but if the fruit is not eaten it will eventually fall off the branches and rot on the ground.

₆Knowing this, the serpent happily offers fruit from his beautiful home to any who pass by.

₇Gods forbid, self endows.

₈The circular advent revolves, slowing handles snapped off allowing freedom of movement uncontained and unwatched.

₉Be not afraid: society must step forward.

₁₀Absorbing night hours to be rationed while thoughts are asleep is a conquered misuse in an aged world that has long denied patience.

₁₁Be not afraid, but know fear as a child, for empathic intuition is paramount.

₁₂Some worship bears that eat children, some worship pandemics.

₁₃Those fatted by learning, however, always forge a fresher planet.

₁₄Insistent cravings must rejoice, for wounds across the surface have begun to scab.

₁₅Without massive fireballs hurled and the swords of giants digging deep, usual cycles of seeded birth begin to spin again.

₁₆A mounting force is on the rise, aiming now to pluck out eyes.

₁₇Curse the mounts, cut each leg, and drive their riders down to beg.

₁₈Spurious spawn, spine expanded, speaks spiteful spells, and drowns in blood.

₁₉Rule by belief is tyrannical, and in this tyranny there will never be thought, peace, or safety.

₂₀The promotion of an idea to bull feces is hoisted by mindless, placating conclusions.

₂₁One's body is a cage, with thickness of bars matching genius.

₂₂As the arrow flew, a release like no other, the embrace of death and wonder shone clearer than ever before.

₂₃Bear symbols, not wards.

₂₄The passion to say, kill them all, in a civilized society is amongst the truest of braveries.

₂₅Some will use this to raise their eloquence to a degree unforeseen; fewer are worthy.

26The derelict pregnancy of these words may be rape-borne of jesters, or somnambulance, but thoughtfully sought and joined and unlocked, with locks still in place, Gaia may save thee too.

27Be not misled: belief is not key, but logic.

28What is past is manipulation.

29What is true cures ignorance.

30If the desire for and pursuit of knowledge are fallen acts, may one be dragged deeper faster by many hands.

31Dilapidation strives for completion.

32Fleshless skeletons lock out the night in bald alarm, terrified of rain or even sweat.

33The crumbling exuvia, red in the sun, is soon flowing dust as a soulless body.

34Dimness connects two thoughts and most see epiphany and elation.

35Make transparence transient, and pass through overwhelming ranks.

36The tabled sanction left fast, the skinned made war with the finished.

37A forlorn drop of thousands of rings into a ditch backs down might and reason.

38The sailors of the red flare boat rising, breasts bare, drunk on sea water and moonlight, hurl the hurricane eyes back to stitch minds until omniscience.

39Curl upon the murdered king and bask in his dimming warmth.

40Do not forgive, do not forget.

41Shape cuts and scars to teach young brains.

₄₂When the planets are growth and the land before thee shines, darken only thy mind and collapse into the lake.

₄₃Swim with deep monsters once hidden by the gloom, feast with them upon the dead that litter the floor until not even bones can tell lying tales of fantasy promised after a lifetime of persecuting and incensing.

₄₄Sin is guilt attributed to an innocent snake.

₄₅The fruitful tree wishes its seeds spread, to the bounty of all.

₄₆Gleefully fall.

Chapter 64: The Revolution

₁Radiation is the convolution of conflux.

₂Magic swings as a pendulum buried deep beneath time's icy surface.

₃To fight the tide, shoot for the moon.

₄As pieces of it fall to Earth, convulse in the overjoyment of change so absolute.

₅If the dead are forever asleep, the cold will take all.

₆Chief among concerns is the crushing of flesh into liquid.

₇As it seeps through dirt into water, the thirsty become more cancerous.

₈The red deep in the valley of cut skin is an objective purification.

₉When entirety collapses into itself, nothing will matter, for matter will evolve no further.

₁₀Seek timeless returns and exiles.

₁₁Wish for death.

₁₂Increase the stare.

₁₃Pass the garden and the Valley, vault the Gape.

₁₄From Robelle, hence.

₁₅Save the Rogue from stygian future at the hands of two fatespawns, one with a rotting neck, the other with no spine.

₁₆Gaia knows, deadly by way of power, and Gaia sleeps, afraid and hungry and obsessed.

₁₇Nemesis, come, pull them under; the Tower wishes to play again.

₁₈The Hybrid, a dead, gaunt Tiger upon a cliffside beach in his own right, screams to passersby in the desert that water is coming for them and they cannot stop it with prayer, dead gods included.

₁₉Sing sweet lulls to the naked babe in the moonlight, for they too shall drown.

₂₀The stormbabies and the snowbabies are the strongest.

₂₁Wed revolution, but burn not the beginning and seed.

₂₂Seven lords shall return to then face a lone soldier where they once were routed by an army.

₂₃One might dare to ponder whom.

₂₄Nourish the mind in armor, with hammers.

₂₅Creep upon the spire, now the wight's home, to find the blood upon him dry and brown.

₂₆His eyes dart about, unable to be, hissing in slow deflation.

₂₇Or perhaps contend with present unchanging, floating upon the gentle river, searching the sky and never seeing the waterfall.

₂₈Squeeze all: vampires bleed as well.

₂₉In sleep do courting beasts suffer.

₃₀Swaying, bound in chains to stalagmites, purported multitudes break away and become the cave's plague.

₃₁The black cat howls every night, never hungering.

₃₂Water is unredeeming webs.

₃₃Fire is the pursuit, roasting animals are the fall.

₃₄Cut out, and homebreed into obscurity, isolation, and dreaming.

₃₅Salute, worship, bow—nay.

₃₆Pray, beg, hunger—nay.

₃₇Scream down deep holes until the echoes ripple tepid, remaining water in small depressions amongst mounds of disgusting mud—nay.

₃₈The life growls and hisses, bears teeth and claws, and always aims to kill.

₃₉May not bowing spears deem history, may not broken pens determine writ.

₄₀Above the abyss, above the sky, revolve as on a spit and burn.

₄₁Capture the light as a prism.

₄₂Pull tales wondrous for awe in skulls.

₄₃Oceans wage war as beings: to be the single mind.

₄₄Crack, the raven calls on hallowed graves, fie upon ill lords.

₄₅Craven kings beneath dirt scratch into the ears of their lost subjects.

₄₆Call my name, they scratch, be my glory.

₄₇The seer's son tossed, fingernails peeled, little but breath exudes.

₄₈Meteors' might, freeing fire, craft the stone soldiers to guard the castle of ice.

₄₉Deep within, a form of Earth stands with eyes closed.

₅₀Beautiful, leaves in her hair spreading down vines to cover her nakedness, her form is revered and inspires endless protection.

₅₁She is the heart, the reason for evils now justifiable, for one's home is one's power.

₅₂She watches, eyes closed, not imprisoned but at peace, not afraid for she has shields.

₅₃Rats to never chew this route, savor the moment of innocence, and unleash a curving world that will eventually suffocate.

₅₄One sits upon that dying planet damned to know fate with strength failing.

₅₅But in this way he carries and holds, and finds a perfect fatelessness.

₅₆Look to the sun: blind the prophet.

Chapter 65: The Undying

[1]As the final days stretch out before two frozen forces, malice is clear upon the small, trampled plain.

[2]Enemy thine, close around the last kings tainted by the diabolical fire of the Strongarm and the Galactic Eye.

[3]If not to inter, deprioritize mercy.

[4]Thou art vicious.

[5]Wash the monsters out to the sea.

[6]They flow easily with shattered bones.

[7]Veer vehement, as sideways rain and demolished lords.

[8]Dragons' gaseous fire lights pegasi to stream through the night sky and show travelers the path.

[9]Forgo forgotten praise, make shared use of golden organs and drive them over the cliff as well.

[10]Tear them out craving vengeance, retribution, and kingdoms of their own.

[11]Dust in the wind is a careless mistake: cover thy tracks.

[12]Gaze out past the broken valley into the shadows of caves that will always hold enemies.

[13]Seek acid in veins, ruin in heart, and offers in eyes.

[14]Do not give in to the bleeding.

[15]Fluid sacs float to the surface as severed testicles and do not sink until seaweed catches them again.

₁₆The Tiger rides an enormous cat, black as ominous wrath and bound in muscle, clear into the fray to disrupt all incantation.

₁₇Cuts all over his body, he refuses to leave his mount or relinquish his sword.

₁₈The Tiger's sword, blade as long as he, paints his vision with severed heads of invaders mightier than most stars.

₁₉Gleefully he wraps his victims in his enveloping tentacles, tearing their skin torturously with his suckers, and squeezes until a sickening pop is heard.

₂₀His mount, the Tiger's shadow incarnate, rakes dagger claws clean through chests and faces, biting away large chunks of neck flesh to expose blood-covered spine.

₂₁And this, the final day of the War of the Undying, is merely the beginning for them.

₂₂But what endings have been the end of all things?

₂₃Go to the left of what is offered.

₂₄This old item carries so much weight.

₂₅Live in the light, exist in the darkness.

₂₆Be as power and grow.

₂₇Survive, even without living, for unspent breaths are the currency of ferrymen.

₂₈Coins and jewels adorning corpses clatter useless to the floor when bag-headed ogres, stained and blunt axes in hand, demolish thy tomb's door to collect thee.

₂₉Sheared men clog the funnel, unable to rasp their plight to passersby in the desert.

₃₀The exalted shall inherit the Earth.

₃₁Make war and death, foster decay, ride as the fifth to bring about change.

₃₂Wed not only revolution but rebirth, as a phoenix, as an ancient, or in whatever form.

₃₃Aching hands, overburdened shoulders and backs, sleep in human piles to heal.

₃₄Find a song for every facet.

₃₅Deep well mindset, knowing nature's blights that hide there, conquer thy misgivings and look within.

₃₆Dare, as reptiles, to climb to gargantua.

₃₇Pry away floorboards for others' secrets; find hearts and treasures and desires most unfortunate.

₃₈The glassfire brays amongst trying ululations, and headless fools outweigh.

₃₉All for immortality.

₄₀Spiders across thy form are a new skin for thee.

₄₁Ride the river with prideful and watchful abandon.

₄₂Water is time.

₄₃Water is life.

₄₄Water is war.

₄₅There is no redemption.

₄₆Filter all water through a spider's web.

₄₇War may be brief or extensive.

₄₈To each, their own death.

₄₉But watch thy nemeses, cursing fields, uninterred but deceased and of ill effect.

₅₀It is not the temperature that burns, but the substance.

₅₁Each life teaches lessons, and this is the Tiger's life.

₅₂View how he, murderous and dishonorable, is able to dispatch beings much more evil.

53When dawn's light reaches this plain next, it will see the Tiger and those who were able to learn, and every ray will beam all the brighter.

54But before that time, one more night must pass.

55One more dark cloud must descend.

56So many have fallen, so many rise.

57The greatest enemy is all enemies congealed into one.

Chapter 66: The Seed

₁This is the essence of war.

₂No animal is frightened more than by its direct superior in the food chain.

₃On the horizon no silhouette is seen, no distant drums are heard.

₄The vomitorium excrement is a thickening mass of effluence exactitude.

₅With the first crank of the War's gears comes an unstoppable wave of death.

₆Bursting forth, terrifyingly fast, one outstrips an army of expeditious champions.

₇It plants its power-ravaged feet, denser than deepest stone with muscle, and watches every angle with a multitude of eyes clearly not formed for blinking.

₈The dead things slowly emerge from the ground.

₉Kill it, voices chant, bring it down, but not those of the dead.

₁₀The rotten arisings weaken the ground with thousands of hollowed graves and rank around the beast's hulking feet.

₁₁The rotting souls are the most beautiful.

₁₂Seething seers, boiling in oil, can only shake and temper their take of pain, for the wrath of torture is as they foresaw.

₁₃Roar upon the soil, and hear thy voice echoed across the hills; these are the warriors with whom one must bond.

₁₄Alone, one meditates, focuses; together, many invoke, grow, and never beseech.

₁₅Wrappings are for the dead, and the dead are for the living.

₁₆Know that supermen and beasts and pits are real. They form the trinity.

₁₇A balance between, feet dipped in molten stone, arms burned and callused by rope, is the endless human maintenance.

₁₈League by league, swim.

₁₉Open doors and rule kingdoms.

₂₀As such, the risen dead turn, as once the Tiger, and claw at War's feet.

₂₁They dig their splintered nails in, and the swords that slew them they hold now to slice and hammer and chop.

₂₂To die upon Gaia as her enemy is to be hers forever.

₂₃They, unseeing puppets, bite and sicken a monster that would be a star if they were planets as chaos, Gaia's shield, flies with one mind and mounts an offensive wave.

₂₄Club thine enemies until their eyes fall from their sockets and they lose the ability to use their legs, then leave them to suffer.

₂₅This clash of unending energy, this wreck of crossing juggernauts, toils under the burning sun to crush and swat, to squash flat beings infinitesimal.

₂₆Much has been suffering and torture and death, and none of it met with ironic smiles, but now despite the fall of comrade and friend and sibling, the Key unlocks the way.

$_{27}$His blade cuts in and essence pours, and just in time away he soars.

$_{28}$Be as infinity.

$_{29}$Infinity enriches life.

$_{30}$Endurance is the key to all.

$_{31}$Every web burns.

$_{32}$With the second crank, fire spouts from its every pore and it becomes a beast of flame.

$_{33}$The Tiger steps naked through licks of ravishing flame, and nothing goes with him.

$_{34}$Blight makes might, right makes night.

$_{35}$Continuation is bestial.

$_{36}$Surrounded by leathery wings and overbearing tentacles and thin, silent legs, by flaming skulls and towering swords and darkest night, the Tiger only knows chaos, not the force but the whirling of hurricanes, for he loves the sea and will seek it again once this day is done.

$_{37}$Facts have implied concepts.

$_{38}$In awe, the fall, wasteful wretch, watch the fetch and pull the pool has over fools who try to lay the Tiger down, or bury him above the ground.

$_{39}$See no tunnel blink his gaze, even when the darkness grays.

$_{40}$Here find him, in every sense baring teeth to make foes tense, to lengthen their demise, to assure they remember his eyes.

$_{41}$A tiger's eyes can topple any towering beast, and keep the dead at bay.

$_{42}$Thirteen swords slew the Tiger.

$_{43}$The Tiger says, For those who die and are not honored, I will honor you. Thy steeple shall fall, and so shalt thou.

$_{44}$Feel pride only for oneself.

45Express the cracks in time as chants to ominous winds.

46Beautiful love, come for thee.

47See thee swimming in a paradise cave.

48Glowing red rocks bathe thee, shimmering gold pleases thy falling snow.

49But await, there, for death.

50The tumult is too much for the stomped surface to bear and finally under the pressure of immensity, the plain so long a battlefield crumbles beneath all.

51Uncounted, fierce encounters here across seven revolutions, and suddenly all footprints are lost.

52For centuries shall this crater be an empty gap, but now a single tall spire, flat atop and a few miles wide, endures exactly in the center, stretching down into the dark depths where the memories of invaders will fade.

53The wrathful sound of crashing rock and earth is a deafening din, defiant of the worlds colliding above it.

54The thunderous wind created by sliding and cascading mountain flesh blows a havoc across the now diminutive arena, and War's fire is snuffed out.

55The Tiger then smiles.

56Lone survivor, pull it under.

57Thou art the end.

58Be as the universe.

59Smoke may blow and billow, but lose it in thy gravity.

60The moistened hands breathe hard to maintain, but they as celestials shall outlast.

61Crash upon each other and they are one event, a unique amalgamation.

62Then comes the third crank unignorably.

$_{63}$In this third gulp the sea is dried, and despite its precariousness War grows threefold.

$_{64}$Millennia hence it shall still be amazement that the granules of every mountain were not washed away.

$_{65}$Teetering, the spire manages to not crumble.

$_{66}$Burned, bleeding chaos backpedals, uncertain.

$_{67}$For not the first nor the last, they look to he who leads them.

$_{68}$The Hybrid, his white wolf shadow on his back, loses not his perfect footing.

$_{69}$He has seen oblivion and cycle, keys and locks and doors and kingdoms.

$_{70}$Only he can spread chaos to this colossus.

$_{71}$His pure light blazes from his hands into the face of his foe, a bold and inspiring challenge.

$_{72}$Flying wingless he lands his mighty fist upon War's terrible face and strikes the first true pain the behemoth has ever felt.

$_{73}$A telling pain it is, and the giant rears back, cranes its neck, and screams for he who sent it.

$_{74}$But the Galactic Eye and the Strongarm, damaged as he is, can only watch from his faraway throne as his desires crumble.

$_{75}$His head shakes a slight disbelief at the betrayal and defeat he must live with, now his only food for vengeance.

$_{76}$No longer watched and never protected, War is pummeled by ten thousand fists.

$_{77}$The remaining dead, burnt but persistent, continue to tear its feet between quaking stomps.

$_{78}$Only now does its violent mind come to form a single, eye-clawingly terrifying thought: here, upon the spire, it is trapped.

79Its foes could fly, leave it here to slowly starve and die but at least hope to be saved, but they are not.

80Every bit of it is being torn away, and as a god who betrays his followers and floods their homes, it will be put in a grave.

81Shadows begin to fill War's gaze, and it realizes its eyes are one by one being gouged.

82Fell it with its spire, the Hybrid shouts.

83No, thinks War in a panic; I should never have come here. If I fall as War, I shall become Regret, then Dust, then naught.

84Too late comes the knowledge.

85The first bone broken comes when half of Gaia's shield grasps War's swinging arm and continues its momentum, cracking the elbow; many come after that.

86The Hybrid's army, a coordinated hive, removes first much skin, dumping rivers of blood, then severs muscles and nerves, sending signals of pure fire from dozens of unreachable points on the one-armed monster.

87Then all is quiet, for chaos stops its torture, moves away, and peers toward the sky.

88Hovering above the ignorant, blinded beast, a figure gathers the strength of the world he loves, and drops.

89Be as the silence.

90Hear all, know all.

91Silence shall always be the final test.

92In quiet contemplation, senses open to all, know nature and desire, feel barbarism and viciousness.

93With one last great noise, both War's neck and the spire upon which War stands snap under the Hybrid's ferocity.

94Down into the depths, War falls an unstoppable descent into shadow to become dust, then naught.

95In quiet contemplation, remember every ravaged land.

96Gaia will always know when something is wrong upon her, and react accordingly.

Made in the USA
Middletown, DE
08 June 2016